Til Death Do Us Part

Felicity Philips Investigates Book 9

Steve Higgs

Contents

1. Loch Richmond Hotel and Spa 1

2. The Scream 8

3. The First Wave 13

4. Not Happening Again 18

5. The Third Wedding Planner 22

6. Gibbering 25

7. The Ceremony 31

8. Lights Out 36

9. Sharing the News 39

10. Stupid Hairstyles 43

11. Victim Number Two 46

12. Dwindling Guest List 52

13. Moving in for the Kill 59

14. True Colours 61

15. Trapped 66

16. Seriously Unpopular   69

17. No Help in Sight   72

18. Running into Trouble   77

19. Improvising Murder   82

20. Soaked   84

21. Wrong Victim   89

22. Worrying Thoughts   91

23. Justin   99

24. Time to Deploy the Pets   101

25. The League   106

26. Think Like a Cat   109

27. No Staff   111

28. Prawns are Better than Humans   120

29. Lies Uncovered   124

30. Paying the Price   127

31. Walking the Righteous Path   130

32. It's a Trap!   132

33. Be One with the Darkness   136

34. Dissension in the Ranks   139

35. The Search for Justin   141

36. Cat Slapped   144

37. Dark Avenger   148

38. No Time to Panic   151

39. Rescue, at Last   155

40. Reunited   156

41. Revealed   161

42. A Perfect Plan Gone Awry   168

43. Contingency Plan   171

44. Human Behaviour   173

45. Between a Fire and a Cold Place   177

46. Trudging Through the Snow   183

47. Standoff   187

48. Aftermath   193

49. Elizabeth Keats   197

50. Epilogue   199

51. Author's Notes: 205

52. What's next for Felicity?   208

53. Free books and more   210

Loch Richmond Hotel and Spa

"This is the place?"

"Yes, my dear." Tim reached across to grip Lydia's hand, glancing with a smile before looking forward again to steer the car down the long drive.

"Oh, it's so beautiful, Tim."

"That is what I promised you, is it not?"

"Yes, but I didn't expect this."

The driveway swept down through a lush green blanket of mature trees toward a lake that stretched to the rolling highlands beyond. Nestled at the water's edge, their accommodation for the weekend, Loch Richmond Hotel and Spa, rose majestically against the picturesque backdrop.

Lydia gave her husband's hand a quick squeeze before releasing it so he could use both to control their hire car. The couple from Toronto, Canada, were in Scotland to attend a conference, but having come all that way, it seemed foolish to fly home without exploring some of the wondrous countryside for which the UK's most northern nation was famous.

Tim received a tip about the hotel and its incredible setting from an old college buddy who happened upon it by accident many years earlier. It wasn't cheap, but Lydia was worth every penny. Mercifully, the winter weather was yet to arrive, though forecasters threatened it would descend any time now.

With that thought in his head, Tim cast his eyes to the horizon where thick clouds were forming. Was there snow in them? The dashboard showed an outside temperature of three degrees. Cool enough, but hardly notable for a Canadian. The real question was whether they would get snowed in. He'd heard it could happen in these parts.

Two miles back, they crossed an old stone bridge which he almost missed. He might have carried on and taken the scenic route had the sat nav not claimed to do so added more than twenty miles and took them all the way around the loch. If the snow came, the bridge would be a problem, as would the steep gradient to get back to it. However, the thought of missing their flight and a few days' work because they were snowed in at a beautiful spa retreat in Scotland did not fill him with dread. Not if he was stuck here with Lydia.

Their ears popped as they descended from the high path to the valley below. It made Lydia giggle, her excitement at the promise of two nights in a luxury spa manifesting in girlish behaviour.

The ancient stone façade of the hotel filled her vision when Tim swung their car past the main entrance and into a parking space.

"That's odd," he remarked, frowning. "Where are all the other cars?"

Lydia tore her eyes from the majestic views. "Perhaps this is the wrong carpark?" she guessed.

"I don't see another one."

"Maybe we have the place to ourselves."

Tim thought that doubtful, but nothing was going to dampen his mood. He killed the engine, opened his door, and went around to open Lydia's like a gentleman from a bygone era. She took his hand and met him with a kiss when she stood.

Arm in arm, they strolled across the gravel and in through the wide oak doors. It was quiet inside, and still, but Tim's rising trepidation quelled when he saw a woman behind the reception desk.

"Hello," he called, a friendly smile fixed on his face.

The woman looked up, but her expression failed to match that of her approaching guests. It wasn't so much that her smile was absent, it was more accurate to say her face would make milk curdle. While it was still in the cow.

She looked to be in her forties but had red lines crossing her cheeks as though she spent much of her life exposed to the elements. Strands of grey peppered her dark brown hair. Also, unlike Tim's wife, who exercised daily and fretted about her figure constantly, the lady eyeing them warily was thick around her hips and bust.

She told them, "Sorry, we're closed."

"Closed?" Tim repeated.

"Yes, closed. You'll have to leave."

Tim's perfectly planned break in the countryside was going up in smoke.

"But we have a room booked. Two nights in one of your suites. I pre-booked spa treatments and paid in advance. How can you be closed?"

"Unexpected circumstances. We failed a food standards inspection. They came yesterday for an unannounced inspection and served notice that we had to evacuate all our guests. I'm terribly sorry, but you *will* have to leave."

"But where will we go?" Lydia asked. The question wasn't necessarily aimed at the woman, but she provided an answer.

"Drive into Richmond. There are bound to be vacancies at the hotels there."

Tim worked hard to control his rising anger. If they were shut yesterday, why hadn't they checked their guest list for new arrivals and sent emails to let people know? How long did they expect to be closed for? Better yet, why wasn't the woman more apologetic? She said the words, but there was no emotional connection to her face. She appeared distracted, nervous even.

He wanted to rant, but knowing no good would come of it, and telling himself the woman delivering the bad news had drawn the short straw, he gripped Lydia's hand and began to back away.

"Come along, darling. There's no point arguing."

The woman behind the reception desk watched the couple leave, her body rigid with fear. They hadn't noticed that her hands never left the counter. Her grip on it was the only thing keeping her upright.

"Well done," said Agatha. Her voice came from a room behind the desk, the door to which swung inward to reveal the petite woman. At five feet four inches the woman was short but not desperately so. Her figure, however, was that of a child, her breasts barely a bump in the woollen jumper she wore. Lines around her eyes showed her thirties were a thing of the past, but no one could deny her attractiveness. Morag wanted to grab a handful of Agatha's lustrous blonde hair and use it to smash her face against the wall.

"I said you would be able to do it, Morag. Now come and join your family."

Morag had to unclench her hands from the countertop, questioning as she did whether her legs would support her.

Impatient, Agatha said, "Oh, do come along, Morag. I made it clear you would all survive this if you are wise enough to do as we say." Agatha offered a reassuring smile Morag didn't believe for a second.

Morag knew she could overpower the petite woman in a heartbeat. She weighed twice as much and had anger on her side plus fear fuelling her adrenaline, but the woman was not alone, and she had leverage.

Morag's husband and two teenage children were in the basement under threat of death by the petite woman's accomplices. Morag had no idea what they wanted – no demands had been made - but they were organised and determined, and above all they were scary.

Led down the back staircase to the basement, relief washed over Morag when she saw her family just as she left them.

"Will there be any more?" asked one of the men. He was tall, thin, and cadaverous with a widow's peak accentuated by his hairstyle which was combed back with product. Morag thought his name was Dutton, but couldn't be sure.

"No," said Agatha. "That's the last of the reservations. There shouldn't be anyone else."

From across the room, another man spoke. "So, that's it until tomorrow?"

Morag thought he looked familiar, and he wasn't the only one she sort of recognised. Four of the men stuck together as if they were a gang and they wore similar haircuts, with long fringes that went out of style twenty years ago.

The petite woman said, "Yes, but that does not mean we can relax. There is much we need to do between now and the ceremony tomorrow afternoon."

Her words acted as a cue to get people moving, and she led the group from the basement. All except the other woman in the group. Like Agatha, who was clearly the group's leader, she was impossibly small. Standing less than five feet tall, the woman, who Morag believed to be called Crystal, was the craziest and scariest of the bunch. Her sparkling blue eyes were like two sapphires, but they hid an incandescent madness Morag hoped she would never see in person. She stopped inside the door, using her presence to trap Morag and her family inside.

Voices echoed back from the corridor outside. "Would it not be easier to kill them now, Agatha?" It came from the tall, cadaverous man.

Holding her breath, Morag doubted she was supposed to hear the response Agatha gave.

"We will kill them when I say it is time. We may yet need them. Remember who brought you into the league, Buttons."

"It's Button," James Button repeated a correction he'd already made more than two dozen times in the last few hours.

"Yeah, okay, Buttons," sniggered Nitro, the lead singer of the long-forgotten boy band, The Mechanics. Passing Button, he aimed an elbow at his midriff, though the blow was teasing and never intended to land.

There were seven of them in total, brought together by a singular desire: revenge. Agatha contacted them separately many months ago, secretly creating a league of patsies who would help her achieve her aim and ultimately take the fall for it so she could walk free.

They had no idea, of course. All too blinded by their own hatred, their blinkered view allowed her to lie to their faces. Well, it would all be over soon. Just another day, and vengeance would be hers.

The Scream

I froze, focussing on what I thought I just heard. Was I wrong?

A scream ripped through the still air.

No, I wasn't wrong. Oh, goody. What disaster had just reared its ugly head?

Buster, my English bulldog, bounced from flat on his back with his paws in the air to fully awake and alert like a chef flipping a particularly rotund pancake.

"*What was that?*" he asked.

My cat, Amber said, "*The sound of a human in distress. They have a desperate need to draw attention to themselves.*"

Buster puffed out his chest. "*Devil Dog is ready to protect the innocent, the weak, and humanity in general.*"

"*Does that mean you are leaving?*"

Buster looked at me. "*Does it?*"

Mindy burst through the door to my room.

"Did you hear that?" My niece is nineteen years old, a qualified martial arts specialist, and my assistant. She is also annoyingly attractive, not least because she has the body of a woman who spends a lot of time exercising and is still in her teens. More often than not, she wears sports gear that accentuates her curves, however her current outfit comprised a Dior dress and bolero jacket. On her feet were four-inch-high Louboutins. I can't wear heels that high for any length of time. They make my feet hurt. But Mindy either puts up with it or simply doesn't suffer the same. They make her calves look great, but I think she does it because she likes to tower over everyone else.

"Yes," I sighed, putting down my makeup brush. My niece doesn't need makeup, she has the freshness of youth on her side. I, on the other hand, have fifty-five years under my belt and need all the help I can get.

My name is Felicity Philips, and I am THE wedding planner. I cater to the rich and famous, planning weddings for celebrities, politicians, and anyone else who is looking to spend a huge amount of money on their nuptials. Don't believe me? Well, I am running the next royal wedding. It's due to take place in just under four months, which might sound like a long time, but to me it is terror-inducingly close.

Mindy kicked off her heels and hitched up her skirt. She wasn't waiting for me and knew I had no option other than to follow. For reasons I cannot fathom, the bulk of the weddings I have managed over the course of the last six months have gone awry. There have been murders, fires, kidnappings, stolen dogs ... the list isn't endless, but it sure feels like it is. Obviously, this has done my reputation no good and each time I attempt to prove the death, drama, and destruction are nothing more than a run of bad luck and in no way to be associated with me, I suffer yet another wedding disaster.

This one was supposed to be different.

I mean, it's in a castle in Scotland for a start. That's hundreds of miles from my home base in the southeast corner of England, but if I hoped the distance might mean the bad luck couldn't find me, it didn't appear to be coming true.

Not if the scream was any indication.

"Come on, Auntie!" Mindy called, sprinting away along the corridor. "I think that was the bride."

Of course it was the bride. It wouldn't matter half as much if it was someone else.

"Come along then, Buster," I picked up my jacket just in case I might end up outside.

"*Oh, good. You are leaving,*" said Amber, closing her eyes again.

"*Why is that good?*" Buster wanted to know.

"Because your snoring was keeping me awake."

"*I wasn't snoring.*"

"You were, actually." I had to side with my cat. "You were snoring quite loudly."

"*As usual.*"

Buster frowned at his feline companion, but contrary to historic behaviour, he didn't strike back with an insult.

"*I'll have you know those weren't snores you could hear. It was the sound of me contentedly purring with the force of a thousand tigers.*"

Amber opened one eye. "*So you're a cat now?*"

Buster tilted his head to one side. "*No. Why would that make me a cat?*"

"Because dogs don't purr, Buster. Cats do. And, for that matter, tigers are cats."

He turned his head to look at me. *"Are they?"*

I flared my eyes at him and stepped into the hallway outside. "I'll explain on the way, Buster."

When he ran past me, I shut my door and ran after my niece, cursing in my head the whole way. The scream had followed the sound of breaking glass. Shattering glass might be more accurate, in fact.

The bride was in the bridal suite, as one might expect, where she would be joined tonight by her groom. The suite was on the top floor overlooking the lake and directly above my room on the second floor. Mindy's room was next to mine, Philippe had the one next to her, and Justin's, that's my master of ceremony, was the other side of him. Justin and Philippe were downstairs in the grand ballroom making final finishing touches to ... well, everything.

We arrived five days ago, getting here well in advance of the event so we could liaise with florists and caterers, make sure the venue was decorated to the bridal party's specifications, and all the other things that have to happen to ensure the big day goes without a hitch.

However, despite a lot of 'what if' planning, I have found I just don't have contingencies in place for when a crazy axe murderer decides today would be a good day to carve his way through the guest list.

Fervently praying that wasn't the precise cause of the bride's scream, I was glad she only felt the need to do it once. Then I realised there could be a good reason why she didn't scream a second time (because the mad axe murderer chopped off her head) and wished she would scream again.

Naturally, Mindy got to the bride's door first, whereupon she knocked and let herself in. When a tirade of shocked expletives failed to follow, I breathed a little easier.

Buster raced ahead of me, proving that he can move fast when he really needs to even though his body looks like a pillow with eyes and feet. Coming from the other direction, members of the bride's family and the groom himself, plus the best man, were all set to get there before me. It meant the room was full by the time I arrived.

The First Wave

"It came through the window," cried Lily, the bride. Wrapped in a thick towelling robe and slumped in an ornate cream and gold armchair, with her bridesmaids fussing around at her feet, Lily's face displayed the shock she felt. The ceremony was set to start in just less than two hours, which is why I had retreated to my room to get ready.

The groom, best man, and father of the bride were all crowded around the object that broke the window. It was a house brick, a somewhat traditional implement for breaking windows if one feels inclined.

The men were raging and talking tough, as men do in such circumstances. The groom stalked to the broken window.

"There's no one out there now," he announced, peering into the gardens. "But they can't have gone far. I'm going out there to find them. Who's with me?"

A chorus of positive replies filled the air. With the groom this weekend were a number of hangers-on - celebrities tend to accumulate those, but most were with Lily. Dean's party consisted almost solely of his business partners, plus his two brothers and their families.

Tailor Ramsey was Dean's longest serving partner. So far as I knew, Dean founded the firm, but to be successful, we all need to include others who will help the business grow. In his late forties, just like Dean, Tailor was the senior partner. Then came Robbie Purcell and finally Oswald Leach, the newest addition to the senior management team and visibly much younger than his longer standing partners.

They all rushed from the room, a herd of men looking to demonstrate their bravery.

More people were arriving at the door, all wanting to know what had occurred and whether anyone was hurt. I knew we wouldn't get a crowd because the wedding is a small, private affair. Their celebrity status meant they could have sold the photographic rights to any number of different celebrity magazines, but the happy couple valued their privacy.

The men didn't stay long, the groom forming a makeshift posse to hunt the grounds for the perpetrator. I did nothing to stop them.

They left the brick behind and when no one else went to pick it up, I chose to inspect it. I am anything but a sleuth. Anyone who knows me will tell you that. There might not be a more hopeless detective on the planet, yet I see little option but to test my lack of natural ability when this is almost certainly the first volley in my latest wedding debacle.

The house brick was just a house brick. Reddish in colour with LBC formed in the centre well on the upper side. I know LBC stands for London Brick Company, don't ask me how, it's just one of those odd bits of trivia I picked up somewhere. It made me question if perhaps that was a clue. Surely, they have brick manufacturers in Scotland. Would they bring bricks up from London to build things here?

Regardless, the more interesting part of the brick was the single word written along both long sides: *Whore*. I find it to be an ugly word that ought to be stricken from the dictionary. That someone aimed it at the bride on her wedding day suggested a serious grudge and not one shred of decency.

Mindy came to stand beside me.

I said, "Don't say it."

She mimed zipping her mouth, very much not saying, 'It's happening again.'

This was to be our last event before the royal wedding, and I so desperately wanted it to go as planned.

Through the broken window, January air spilled to chill the room, and with it the voices of the men searching the grounds outside. I walked over to look out.

With a breath to centre myself, I pushed all negative thoughts from my head and went to the bride. No matter who attends a wedding and regardless of who is picking up the bill, the bride will always, always, always be the focal point. That is how it has always been, and it will never change on my watch. Unless it's a gay wedding. Obviously.

I had to walk around the ladies filling the room to get to Lily, but when I got there I discovered why I hadn't seen or heard Buster since I arrived. He was upside down at the bride's feet getting tummy tickles from three different women.

"*I'm providing stress relief*," he sighed contentedly, his tongue lolling from the side of his mouth to hang in free air.

Addressing the bride, I said, "Lily, do you have any idea who would want to do this?"

She looked up at me, her face radiating innocence. "None at all, Felicity. It's very hurtful, but I think it must be a mistake. Like they threw it through the wrong window."

Her two bridesmaids chipped in to back her up.

"Everyone loves Lily," said Tamara.

"She's never made an enemy in her life," agreed Chastity.

All three were in their very late twenties and had known each other since they went to the same preschool in the same village. They were from Eccles, a village a few miles outside of Rochester, which was how they knew of my boutique and the service I offered.

Moving on to the question I really wanted to ask, I said, "Lily, what do you want to do? We can delay the ceremony if you want more time to prepare. We can ..."

"No!"

I was going to say we could proceed as planned if she felt able, but Lily made her feelings clear.

"I'm marrying Dean exactly as we have planned. At the time we set, in the place we chose, with the people we love around us. No one and nothing is going to stop that."

I nodded. "Very good. Then I think we should get someone in to patch the window and get everyone but the bride and bridesmaids out." I thought I might have to clap my hands to get people moving, but they began to drift toward the door. Mindy held it open for everyone to leave.

"Come along, Buster. That means you too."

"*Awww.*"

Not Happening Again

I needed to go back to my room to finish getting dressed, but I wanted to see if the men had found anything in their hunt for the culprit. I could take Buster outside for a little 'exercise' at the same time.

"Shall I come with you, Auntie?"

"No, Mindy. It's best if you get ready, but if you could track down the facility manager and get the window patched, that would be enormously helpful."

She dashed away with the enthusiasm only a teenager can muster, calling over her shoulder, "I'll get right on it."

At the bottom of the stairs, I ran into Justin. Justin is in his forties and married with two children. Lean and average height, he also has average looks but wears fabulous suits that make him stand out. He is also one of those people who is brimming with natural confidence which makes him a natural for his job. Specified by the bride and groom, he wore a pseudo military outfit in black with bold red stripes up the legs and gold brocade across the epaulettes.

"Is there a problem?" he asked. "I just saw the groom in the grounds with half the other male guests."

I told him about the house brick and saw the concern clouding his brow.

"It's not happening again," I hissed through my teeth.

"No, Felicity, of course not. I wasn't thinking anything of the sort."

"How is everything down here? The bride insists the ceremony will proceed on time."

"We're about ready. A few last details in the kitchen, but they have hours to get ready to serve the wedding breakfast."

One of the things I like most about Justin, and probably the reason I have been working with him for so many years, is his absolute unflappability. He is never not calm. Concerned occasionally. Possibly even worried at times, but never anxious. I could feel his calm radiating into me.

I patted his arm to show how much I appreciated him and aimed my feet in the direction of the exit.

Richmond Castle isn't really a castle at all, but a very nice stately home built in the sixteenth century. Wide sweeping staircases, ornate stonework around every door and window, both inside and out, plus gargoyles on the eaves of the roof, and wonderful oak fittings throughout, made it as picturesque as a Scottish castle can possibly be.

This was my first visit. Though known as a famous wedding location, it booked up more than a year in advance if you wanted a weekend ceremony. Now on my fifth day at the venue, I knew my way around well enough that I could navigate to the nearest exit. On this occasion, I went through the library.

The temperature dropped like an anvil the second I stepped outside. Artificially warm inside the castle, in the grounds it could not be more than one or two degrees. Thick black clouds were overhead, threatening rain. Inclement weather is never desirable at a wedding, but the bride and groom knew what to expect in Scotland in January and were lucky there wasn't a foot of snow already.

Everything would take place inside, so it could rain as hard as it wanted today and no one would care.

Buster wasted no time finding a bush to 'water' and I left him to explore while I made a beeline for the groom's party. Not that I really had to go to them, they were already on their way to me.

"Does that lead inside?" Dean pointed at the door behind me, guessing I had just come through it.

"Yes. It opens into the library. Did you find anything?"

Dean shook his head. "Whoever threw that brick must have launched it and snuck away. Can you vouch for all the staff here?"

I could not. The castle had its own staff, many of whom were employed specifically on weekends to cater wedding events. We had brought some of our own people, but the kitchen staff, wait staff, cleaners, fixers, gardeners ... they were not people I knew. But why would any of them have a grudge against Lily? Unless it was to do with her fame.

The groom, Dean Coolidge, made his fortune as a record producer, leaping to global fame when asked to host a TV show looking for new singing talent. Lily was one of contestants who did not win the first season, but she was the one who succeeded after the show was done.

When I questioned if the brick could be connected to her pop stardom, Dean huffed an exasperated breath. The kind that makes your lips flap.

"Who can say? Lily receives less hate mail than anyone I have ever worked with, but she does get some. Anyone who puts their head above the parapet attracts a few crazies. A few haters. Maybe that's all this is." He sighed and looked annoyed, hands on hips, kicking at the grass with his shoe. "I should have organised security."

"I'm sure that won't be necessary," I replied, praying I wouldn't be proven wrong. Changing the subject, I said, "I spoke with Lily, and she is determined the ceremony will go ahead as planned." I shot my cuff to check the time. "That gives us just less than two hours. I'm sure you chaps won't need long to get ready, but a pre-wedding drink is close to a tradition. Especially in these parts."

My suggestion was received with enthusiasm, the father of the bride clapping the groom on the shoulder and offering to buy the first round.

Telling myself everything was back on track, I was about to go back inside when the unmistakable sound of something exploding boomed across the castle grounds.

The Third Wedding Planner

E lizabeth Keats watched from a hunting hide two hundred yards from the castle. Through her binoculars she saw the stunned expression on Felicity Philips' face and basked in the joyful warmth it brought her.

"Take that, you dirty, underhanded cow."

The brick through the window was a good start, but it was nothing more than that. She needed to make them believe there was a psycho stalker after the bride, but to make them take the threat seriously and be sure they aborted the wedding, Elizabeth set fire to the bride's car.

All it took was a pry bar to force the petrol cap open, a length of rag, and a box of matches. It was ridiculously easy, stupidly cheap, and she found all kinds of advice online to make sure the car didn't explode while she was standing next to it.

Scanning back across the castle, she saw faces pressed to the windows, the wedding guests and staff all gawping at the spectacle in the carpark. She had watched the groom along with the wedding's male contingent scurry around the castle grounds looking for who could have thrown the brick, but they were never going to find her. Not that they would think she could be the culprit. If anyone approached her, they would find a woman on a walking holiday. Only Felicity would recognise her, but that was okay because Elizabeth was in Scotland to kill her business rival.

First, Elizabeth revealed to the world the sordid truth about Primrose Green. Watching her fall from glory when the racy photographs she leaked went viral was more fun than she could have imagined, but she never once believed the royal family would then give the wedding contract to Felicity Philips. What were they thinking?

It made her very angry, but only for a short while. When she calmed down, her rational side returned and with it the ability to plot. The papers snapped up the story about Primrose, and though Felicity hadn't been foolish enough to pose naked alongside male models, there was still the run of failed weddings to feed them.

Elizabeth had no clue why Felicity's weddings were going sideways and didn't much care. The why of it wasn't important. It made a juicy story, and the papers ran with it, calling her the Wedding Doomer. Incredibly, when the story broke, the royal family didn't sack her as they had Primrose, which made no sense whatsoever. Never one to be perturbed, Elizabeth simply doubled down with a plan that couldn't fail.

She was going to kill Felicity. That would leave the royal wedding without a planner, and she was poised to fill the spot.

Misdirection, that was the point of attacking the bride. Everyone would be looking her way, so when Felicity met her end, the world would assume her death was nothing more than collateral damage.

Elizabeth continued to watch, entertained by the ensuing panic. The question now was whether she had overdone it and scared the bride into calling off the wedding. That wouldn't be insurmountable, but it was better if the wedding guests didn't now all jump in their cars and run for the hills. If they left, Felicity might also leave, and that would ruin things.

However, knowing Felicity as she did, Elizabeth expected the ceremony to go ahead. So she watched, ready to react to whatever situation arose.

Gibbering

I couldn't see the explosion, but I felt it. As did Buster. My bulldog flattened himself to the lawn, tucked his tail between his legs, and squashed his ears tight against his skull. Until he realised people could see him cowering. At that point, he jumped back to his full height and glared in the direction of the blast.

A shockwave of air swept across the lawn, flattening it, and birds took to the air when the trees deflected outward as though pressed by an invisible hand. It took my breath, snatching it from my lungs even as the sound hit the distant hills and bounced off, echoing through the silent valley like an insult.

The men and Buster all ran around the side of the castle, looking for the source of the explosion. However, I was stunned, and my legs refused to work for several seconds. I genuinely considered just getting in my car and driving home. I could call it quits, give up being a wedding planner, and slide into early retirement many years before I was due. It upset me a little that I knew I would never forgive myself if I chose the defeatist route, but right in that moment, I felt beaten.

"Felicity? Are you okay?" I turned to find Justin hurrying my way. He was coming from the library, and I guess he'd spotted me through the window to know where I was.

The sound of his voice unfroze my legs, allowing me to move, and though it conflicted with common sense, I went after the men. The boom had already faded to nothing more than echoes, yet the castle grounds were anything but quiet as shouts of outrage, fear, panic, and screaming filled the air.

Mercifully, the screaming wasn't due to injury, but a result of the shocking and unexpected event. With Justin at my side, I rounded the building to find a Mini Cooper, the bride's Mini Cooper to be exact, burning with ferocity. Surrounding it, but at a safe distance, were the groomsmen, the groom, the father of the bride, and just arriving were a glut of castle staff, two of whom were carrying fire extinguishers.

Dutifully, the two men rushed forward, racing to get to the car only to be halted by the invisible wall of heat coming from it. I watched them bravely discharge the extinguishers, but it was much akin to throwing jelly at a speeding Volvo and thinking it might be sufficient to make it stop.

"Felicity?" Justin touched my arm.

I hadn't answered his previous question and now I was staring at the burning car with disbelieving eyes and my mouth hanging open. Twisting from the waist, I stared at him, my mouth and expression unchanged.

"It's happening again," I gibbered. I wish to claim that I have never knowingly gibbered in my life. Nor have I raved, burbled, or howled at the moon, but I felt disconnected from the sane world and questioned if I might be about to start dribbling. It *was* happening again. Despite all my planning. Despite going hundreds of miles away from my home county where all the other dramas had unfolded. Despite telling myself the wedding disasters of the last few months were nothing more than an unlucky streak, it was happening again.

Someone was targeting the bride, and yet another wedding was about to go up in smoke.

Smoke? Ha-ha! Nice one, Felicity, the bride's car is on fire.

I sniggered.

"Felicity?" Justin said my name again, this time questioning the madness in my eyes.

The first few drops of a light drizzle pattered down on and around me.

I snorted a laugh.

Justin said, "Um. Is there something I'm missing?"

"It's raining," I pointed out, my words tinged with laughter that bordered on hysteria. "It will put the fire out."

"I think perhaps we should get you inside." Justin put an arm around my shoulders to guide me.

I guess he expected my feet to move, but they didn't budge. I was staring at the bridal party, wondering whether one of them might be to blame. It wasn't always the case that someone close to the happy couple was behind it all, but it had proven to be exactly that enough times for me to look at them first.

The bride wanted to get married today. The brick through her window only strengthened her resolve. I doubted the exploding car would change anything.

"Mrs Philips!" Lily's voice cut through the fog of confusing thoughts clogging my brain.

I looked up to find her hanging out of her broken bedroom window. There were men either side of her; castle staff in overalls undoubtedly there to patch over the hole. At this distance I couldn't tell for sure, but it looked at though she was crying. What normal person wouldn't be under such circumstances?

"Mrs Philips, I want to get married right this second! Can you make that happen, please? I don't care if things aren't ready. I'm doing it before whoever is behind this can do anything else."

"What about your car? We need to call the police."

"I have already made the call," said a voice to my half right.

I turned to find Kerry Kirby, the castle manager, heading my way. He had his phone up to his left ear and appeared to be listening. Broad across the shoulders and narrow in the waist, he wore a kilt at all times and looked capable of tossing a caber over the castle if the need arose. His trimmed but bushy beard bore traces of ginger that did not extend into his mop of brown hair, and he had the greenest eyes I have ever seen.

"They are already on their way," Kerry advised. "We can exshpect them within the hour." His Scottish lilt, the way he sounded so much like Sean Connery, just melted me. His accent probably did nothing for him among the local women but take him out of Scotland and he would need a stick to beat the women away.

"That long?" I questioned, shocked to hear they were in no hurry.

"It is more than thirty miles to the nearest police shtation, Mrs Philips, and there are no motorways between here and there. To get here in an hour will be good going."

From her window, Lily shouted, "That gives us enough time to complete the ceremony. Let's get on with it!"

A cog dropped into place inside my head and just like that I was back in control. I had a purpose. I had direction, and I knew exactly what I needed to do.

Raising my voice to be heard as the drizzle shifted from first gear to second, I shouted back, "Absolutely. I will gather the wedding party and assemble them in the chapel. A few minutes is all I need." I wanted to suggest she take as long as she needed for hair and makeup, but her opinion that we should delay not one second longer than necessary was a policy I could fully endorse. If I could just get the ceremony in the bag, I could claim success.

Well, provided the culprit didn't then murder the bride and groom in their marital bed. Forcing that terrible thought from my mind, I called for Buster and started walking with such determination in my step that I left Justin in my wake.

He ran to catch up. "I'll get to the chapel and make sure the vicar is ready."

"Please do." I loved his ability to assess what I needed before I had to ask. "I will send Mindy to guide the bride and her bridesmaids while I gather the guests and get them into position." The groom chose that moment to look my way. A simple hand gesture was all I needed to get him moving to the castle. "If you please, gentlemen," I added. "You all heard the bride."

"I'll swing by the kitchen and let them know we are going early," said Justin. "They ought to be able to get the canapes finished and ready to serve even if the guests have to wait for dinner."

He peeled off, and I let him go, confident there was no need to check his tasks would be done. The men were heading inside, encouraged by the rain which continued to pick up speed. I followed them through the open door, the father of the bride displaying old school manners in holding it for me.

"Hurry now, if you please, gentlemen," I called at their backs. "Let's not keep the lady waiting." My encouragement was almost certainly unnecessary, they were hustling at a jog already. Paused in the open doorway, I took a moment to myself.

This wedding could be a success. The bride and groom deserved their day, and I was going to give it to them.

A crack of distant thunder echoed across the landscape to punctuate my positivity like a death knell.

The Ceremony

I took Buster back to my room where I settled him on a blanket in the corner by the window.

Thunder boomed like the sound of distant guns. Distant guns that threatened to come oh so very much closer.

Amber opened an eye. "*Please tell me that wasn't the dog.*"

"There's a storm coming, Amber."

Buster paused midway through his three rotations on the blanket. "*You praise me with your suspicions, you know that, cat? Any dog that could fart loud enough to rattle the masonry would be the toast of the town.*"

"*Mm-hmmm. And you think that is a good thing?*"

I had no time to spare on their discussion. Leaving them to argue, I backed out the door, made sure it locked behind me, and hurried to round up the wedding guests.

Heading to the chapel, I picked up the sound of Philippe chatting. Philippe is a makeup artist I 'accidentally' hired when my mouth got away from me. I didn't really have a use for him at the time, but landing the royal wedding contract increased my workload significantly. I'm not using his makeup skills, but he seems thankful for the regular wage. He's a lovely boy, and I like him on the team, but he can get distracted, and I must have told him to stay off his phone a hundred times.

"Philippe."

The sound of his name coming from my mouth sent a spasm through his body. He said something quickly, ended his call with a hasty kiss, kiss, and tried to pocket it so I wouldn't see.

"Mrs Philips," he greeted me with a smile. "I was at a loose end. Is there anything I can be getting on with?"

I held out my hand. "Give it to me, Philippe." I have a simple rule about phones at weddings: there are none. Not when it applies to my team. No one else challenges my policy, but I catch Philippe all the time.

He pulled a sad face, but produced the phone and placed it in my palm.

"It was just one call."

I doubted that was true.

"You can have it back after the wedding breakfast. Until then, I need you focused on the bride and groom and everything happening around you."

"Yes, Felicity."

I hurried him to the chapel where Justin met me at the door.

"That's almost everyone," he said, one hand in the air as he performed a head count.

"Do you have a pocket for this?" I asked, offering him the phone. It wouldn't fit in my handbag.

Justin glanced down, raised an admonishing eyebrow at Philippe, who had the decency to look ashamed, and took it from my unresisting palm. The phone went into an inside jacket pocket where it would remain warm and safe until much, much later.

Two minutes later, the tiny chapel was about full. Men were still trying to tie their ties, one chap ran through the doors tucking his shirt tails into his trousers, and I spotted another with no shoes. Defying gender stereotypes, the women were dressed and made up. Possibly this was because they started two hours before the men even thought about getting started, but apart from one or two who looked to have abandoned their makeup routines halfway through, the ladies were coming out on top.

The final guests through the door were Oswald and Robbie. Justin ushered them to the last available seats in the back row.

I had already counted the guests, ticking them off by name from the list in my head, but allowed myself an additional twenty seconds to count them again before raising my thumb to show the vicar we were ready to get underway.

Reverend Hector Malice couldn't be a day under sixty, which is to say I felt certain he ought to have retired from the clergy more than a decade ago and was almost certainly closing in on seventy-five. That's not to say I doubted his ability or authority to conduct the service. More to the point is that he was utterly unflustered by the dramatic events unfolding in his parish or the sudden change in timing that demanded his immediate reaction. He was tubby and bald, with just a few wisps of white hair clinging to his scalp, but he looked the part and would guide the congregation through the service with practiced ease.

With a nod from the vicar, the organist began to play 'Love Divine' a traditional wedding anthem I could recite the words to with no need to be conscious.

Reverend Hector met my eyes, a silent indication that he was ready, and I turned to look back through the doors to Mindy. My niece held the bridal party in check, ready for my signal it was time for Lily to make her grand entrance.

Not quite yet. All the pieces were in place, but there was no need to hurry things. Not now. We had hurried enough.

Mindy raised her eyebrows in question, and I gestured that she should wait, giving her a smile that spoke of calm and patience. All was good. On edge for the last hour, though truth be told I'd been fighting my anxiety since before I left home almost a week ago, I was finally settled. This was where I felt at home. I took a deep breath and told myself it was okay to relax.

I gave it a full minute. Long enough for the organist to play two verses and the chorus before I signalled the vicar again. The moment he looked at the organist, I motioned that Mindy should start the bride and her father. The bridesmaids would trail after, but a younger female relative throwing petals would not precede her, for none existed on either side.

The organist flowed seamlessly from 'Love Divine' into 'The Wedding March' and the congregation in the chapel twisted as one to see the bridal party enter.

My work for now essentially complete, I stepped into the pew to my left and faced forward, watching impassively from the back of the room as my slick operation did me proud. Lily drew level with me, giving a sideways glance and a nervous grin that told me her thoughts were where they were supposed to be: on her imminent nuptials, not the psycho out there hoping to ruin her wedding.

I watched her reach the front of the aisle where her father stepped to one side and left her standing alongside her husband to be.

Outside the rain fell, a constant background drumming no one could hear above the organ.

Until the power went out and we were all plunged into almost total darkness.

Lights Out

A woman to my far left screamed, her voice rebounding off the walls and ceiling after she silenced herself in an abrupt, embarrassed manner. Mutterings arose, and I heard a few renditions of, "Now what?".

However, before the voices could gather any momentum, Reverend Hector said, "Not to worry, it's just the storm tripping the breakers. It won't take me a moment to reset it. James?" he addressed the organist. "Can you light some candles, please?"

The sudden lack of overhead light threw the chapel into darkness, but the sun was still up outside, and my eyes quickly adjusted to the dim light level. Had there not been a weather front in the valley, bright sun would stream through the stained glass behind the altar. Instead, we settled for something better than total darkness until candles sparked into life.

"Shouldn't take but a moment for the vicar to reset the power," advised James the organist. "It's not unusual for it to go out."

He moved around the chapel, his passage trackable more by the pinpoints of flames coming to life than any ability to see him.

Keeping a lid on my frustration, I focused on my breathing. This was nothing. A minor setback that would be resolved momentarily.

Except it wasn't.

Mindy's question echoed my thoughts when she said, "He's been gone a while." She'd slipped in next to me after the bridal party passed and had been quiet ever since, but she wasn't wrong.

I checked my watch, cursing myself for not marking the time when the lights went out. How long had it been? It felt like it had to be five minutes now, but was it more than that? Or less?

The guests were whispering, light from various people's phones illuminating the chapel's darkened interior far more than the candles. Shortly, their comments would rise in volume, and when they wanted someone to resolve the problem, they would only look one way.

Embracing my role with a silent groan, I had to unclench my jaw to say, "I am just going to check if the vicar needs a hand." I heard more than one person say something like, "About damned time," as I made my way down the aisle, past the bride, to whom I whispered a heartfelt word of encouragement, and out through the same door through which Reverent Hector passed a few minutes earlier.

Mindy was with me, glued to my shadow as if I had any idea where I was going. Only now that I was in a corridor beyond the back of the chapel did I think to question where the vicar had gone. I knew my way around the castle, but not this part of it. I was looking for a breaker box and guessed that would be tucked in a maintenance room somewhere. Why hadn't I asked James the organist where I needed to go? Or better yet, dragged him with me as a guide? Too late now. To go back to the chapel would make me look incompetent and stupid, so I pressed on, using the light on my phone to illuminate the way as I checked every door until I found the right one.

How could I tell it was the right room? Because the vicar was in it.

I didn't bother to ask him if he was struggling to get the power back on. There seemed little need since he was very clearly dead.

Sharing the News

"**W**ow!" said my niece. "Auntie, that was some good swearing and I've dated a soldier."

Had I employed bad language? I genuinely couldn't say if any words had left my mouth or not, and I really didn't care.

The vicar was lying on the stone floor in front of me, his cassock spread out to either side to give him the appearance of a flattened shuttlecock. One could be fooled into thinking he had died of natural causes such as a heart attack were his head not on back to front. His sightless eyes and shocked expression, despite the unnerving fact that he was lying chest to the floor, were probably what sparked the tirade of curse words my niece insisted I recently spewed into the world.

I could see him only by the light from my phone, but that was more than enough to convince me the bride's psycho fan had escalated their terror spree another notch.

"Auntie, what do we do? We should try to get the power back on, right?"

Power meant light, which would allow me to see the vicar in all his gloriously murdered detail. Of course, it would also illuminate all the dark corners in which his killer might still be hiding.

"Yes, Mindy. Power would be good," I hedged.

My niece touched my shoulders as she stepped around me and it gave me great comfort to know how well she could handle herself if there was a killer anywhere nearby. Witness to her battling criminals before, it would surprise me not one bit if Mindy ripped off an attacker's testicles and proceeded to beat him to death with them, just to get his attention.

Apart from blood, we really didn't have a whole lot in common.

"Um, Auntie, I think the power is off for good."

The light from her phone shone on what even I could see was a set of breakers. They were smashed, quite literally, to pieces. A sledgehammer sat on the ground next to what had once been a service unit. Parts of cables poked out at the top and shards of the plastic case, in which the connections once sat, littered the floor. No one was getting the power back up in the next few days, let alone the next few hours.

Terror shoved frustration out of the way as it barrelled into a dominant position at the front of my brain. It was one thing to throw a brick through a window with an insult on it. That was cowardly and faceless. Setting fire to a car was a distinct step further down the insanity scale, but now we had a murderous saboteur in our midst, and I couldn't guess what they might try next.

"Mindy?"

"Yes?"

"Can you take me back to the chapel, please? I think we need to get everybody out of here."

All credit to my niece, she didn't hesitate. She also made a big point of covering my back.

Getting back to the chapel took only a few seconds, though I could feel danger creeping up my spine the whole way. Coming back through the door to the right of the altar, every eye in the congregation looked my way. The pressure of the news I held weighed upon me like an anchor, but there was no option to keep it a secret.

"Is everything all right?" asked the groom as he advanced. The best man came with him, their faces displaying concern. "Does the vicar need a hand?"

"Um." How to answer that one? I didn't want to cause a panic, but I also felt it would be a good idea for everyone to pack their bags and head for home. Getting close to the groom and his best man, I leaned in so our heads were almost touching. "I'm afraid the electricity supply has been sabotaged and the vicar has been murdered."

"Murdered!" Dean blurted at a volume loud enough to ensure even Lily's ageing and rather deaf grandmother would hear.

"Yes," I sighed. "That's why I whispered it."

The entire front row of the chapel were descending on me and those in the pews behind were shuffling to the ends to do the same.

A thousand questions erupted into the air at once, but despite the cacophony of noise, I heard Lily's wail. Through the press of bodies demanding answers, I saw her face crumbling. Tamara and Chastity were with her, giving what comfort they could, but there was no rescuing the situation now.

"Are you sure?" asked someone. "I'm going to check," said someone else and before I knew it people were streaming through the door to find the vicar's body.

Fruitlessly, I called after them, "Don't touch anything! The police will need to see it as it is." They paid me no heed, rushing from the room only to report their findings with cries of shock and horror a few moments later.

Left with the groom and some of the bride's immediate family, I said, "I think we should evacuate the chapel and move to somewhere brighter and more central until the police arrive."

Lily wailed her objection, "But we're supposed to be getting married!"

I had to force my way through the crowd a little to get to her. Taking her hands in mine, I had no trouble sounding disappointed when I said, "I'm sorry, Lily. I can overcome most obstacles, but for the ceremony to be official we do need a minister."

"Can't you get a new one?" She was being serious.

Fortunately, her intended stepped in, pulling her into an embrace to whisper soothing words. The wedding was off. There would be no ceremony, no banquet, and no speeches. Lily's success had brought her many things, and today its gift was grief.

Behind us, the guests who went to see the vicar for themselves were returning. Their faces were white, and their expressions were dour. No one had anything much to say.

Raising my voice, I addressed everyone in the chapel, "Ladies and Gentlemen, I believe we should all retire to the castle's banquet hall and the bar there. The police will have questions for us when they arrive."

Stupid Hairstyles

Agatha was impatient by the time Turbine and Diesel returned. She hated them and the other two, Nitro and Sparks. All four were members of a boy band that rode high in the charts for more than a year before plummeting into obscurity just as quickly. That they kept their stage names and refused to be known by what was on their birth certificates spoke volumes about their mentality. They were feeble-minded cretins, but they harboured the same thirst for vengeance that drove her and that made them allies.

"Is it done?" she demanded.

Turbine tried to go around her to get into the building. On the way back from the castle, the rain came so hard they were both drenched to the skin, yet she blocked his path and looked quite unmoveable despite her diminutive size.

Snippily, he grunted, "Yes, Agatha, it is done."

Still she didn't move. "Exactly as I told you?"

Getting annoyed, Diesel shoved Turbine ahead of him to get under cover. "Yes, Agatha. We smashed the fuse box and waited for the vicar to show up. When he did, we killed him and left him to be found."

"Yeah, we even hung around to make sure someone found him," added Turbine. "That was risky, you know. Getting caught isn't part of the plan."

"It was only risky because the pair of you are absolute idiots. How can you even see where you are going with those ridiculous hairstyles."

"These are our trademark. The hair sets us apart from the other boy bands."

"But you're in your forties! You're not a boy band! For crying out loud, Nitro is going bald and has a beer belly!"

"We've still got a loyal fan following, you know," Diesel defended their beliefs.

Agatha pinched the bridge of her nose and lifted her right hand, palm out to stop them from saying anything else.

"I don't care, okay? All I meant is that you have been out in the rain and your hair is hanging over your eyes."

Turbine and Diesel turned their eyes upward, trying to see their hair. Failing, Turbine twisted to look at his partner.

"Dude, your hair is ruined!"

"So's yours!"

Overwhelmed with panic, they shoved past Agatha to get to a mirror. Rolling her eyes, she followed, glad they would soon be dead.

She passed them a moment later, both men standing hip to hip and nudging each other to check their reflections in the narrow mirror. Agatha left them behind. The next part of the plan had to be executed precisely if she hoped to be victorious. The police would be on their way, of that she held little doubt, but their involvement would complicate things, so it had to be stopped.

Far from being a hurdle, the challenge presented her with an opportunity. She needed the wedding guests scared enough to abandon the castle, and they were well on their way to doing just that.

Victim Number Two

I thought getting everyone from the chapel to the bar would be a relatively simple task. The vicar's murder left no question the wedding was off while simultaneously providing a viable excuse for day drinking.

Justin was at the back of the chapel already – one motion from me was all he needed to open the door and be ready to lead the way.

However, when I got the guests around me aimed in the general direction of the exit at the back of the chapel, one of the groom's business partners confronted us. Oswald Leach stood in the middle of the aisle, his mouth opening and closing. No words came out, but the look of horrified shock on his face made my stomach tighten.

Dean asked, "Ossie? Are you okay?"

To answer, Oswald raised his hands. His bright red hands that were dripping with blood.

"He's dead!" Ossie blurted. Casting his eyes to the right, he looked at another of the record company executives. Dean was the figurehead, the name people knew, but his top tranche of colleagues were here for his wedding, making merry in the opulent surroundings.

"Wait," Dean started forward with faltering steps. "That's ... that's Robbie."

Oswald turned his head to look our way again. "He's dead," he repeated. "Someone stabbed him. I thought he was asleep, he's had a few, so I grabbed him and ..." Oswald stared at his hands.

A scream ripped through the room, the news spreading to add fuel to the panic already bubbling in the background. I felt like joining in. First the vicar, and now one of the guests. What next?

As though someone hit the play button, people started moving all at once. Some went straight out the chapel door, escaping without a glance at the latest body. Others, including the groom, went to Robbie. They checked his pulse, confirming he was indeed expired, and stood looking at each other with bewildered faces.

The bewilderment did not, however, last very long. Mere seconds after Oswald's announcement, the accusations began.

"You were sitting next to him, Ossie," Tailor jabbed a finger at his partner's gut. "Are you seriously expecting us to believe you saw nothing? Someone stabbed him right next to you!" I knew nothing about the office dynamic, but it sounded like Tailor was happy to point the finger at Oswald. "You know what?" he asked. "I think you did it."

Oswald's eyes bugged from his head. "What?"

Tailor got in his face. "You never liked him. Everyone knows that."

"That doesn't mean I killed him!"

"Oh, yeah?" Tailor showed his teeth. "Empty your pockets."

"What?"

"You heard me!" Tailor looked ready to throw a punch.

Dean stepped between them, pushing Tailor away before turning to Oswald. "Just do it, Ossie. That's the easiest solution."

I thought Oswald was going to argue, but after a moment where he argued with himself, he shrugged, removed his jacket, and showed that all he had was a wallet, a phone, a handkerchief, and some loose change.

"Happy?" Oswald snapped at Tailor.

"My friend was just murdered, Ossie," Tailor growled. "I am anything but happy, and you're not off the hook yet. Everyone, look around. He must have stashed it somewhere."

Now over his initial shock, Ossie was swift to respond. "You're crazy. How do we know you didn't do it?"

Tailor scoffed, "I was on the other side of the aisle, stupid. How could I have done it without anyone seeing me?"

"The lights were out," Oswald pointed out with a triumphant grin. "No one would have seen you moving about."

"Why you …" Tailor rushed to get to Oswald, the sudden violence drawing fresh gasps and cries of alarm from the guests still in the chapel.

Dean caught him, Lily's father lending his weight to keep a punch from being thrown, but it was the bride who ended the argument.

"Stop it!" she screamed at the top of her lungs. "Stop it, all of you!"

Dean shoved Tailor away, his face leaving no doubt there would be consequences if he persisted.

Lily was a bawling mess. The speed at which we attacked the ceremony, foolishly thinking that would overcome any dastardly plans Lily's evil fan might want to cook up, meant her hairdressing never took place. The bridesmaids did their best with it, but it was far from the elaborate styling she picked out. Her makeup was either gone or being worn in a mess down her cheeks and around her chin. She had a drop of snot hanging from the tip of her nose.

It is entirely possible that I have never seen a more unhappy bride.

Dean swept her into his arms, lifting her from the floor to carry her away from the carnage that was their wedding day. I heard him ask where she wanted to go, and her reply that she wanted to be alone. It sounded like the perfect thing to do were there not a killer on the loose.

"Sorry," I touched Dean's arm as he came past me. "Is that really the best idea? Shouldn't we all stay together until the police get here?"

Lily's father chimed in, "That would be the safest thing to do, my cherub."

Dean looked disappointed to agree, but said, "Whoever this is does seem to be after you, my love. I would feel safer if you were in my sight."

Lily thrashed to get out of his arms. "Don't you think I know that? Don't you think I know your friend is dead because of me?"

"Well, that's not quite what I meant …"

Lily shut Dean up by screaming in his face. "This is all your fault! You made me famous! You were the one who told me I would be adored by millions of fans."

Very much on the back foot, the groom tried to defend himself. "You are adored by millions of fans, Lily."

"Yes! But some of them are insane! Do you think my car would explode if I worked in the supermarket? Would the vicar be murdered on my wedding day if I had a job driving a bus?"

Dean opened his mouth to respond, only to shut it again when Lily slapped him. It made a 'crack' sound like a batsman driving the ball through the slips to the boundary. The groom and everyone around him looked stunned.

Lily swung another, but this time Dean ducked it, which turned out to be the wrong thing to do. Lily threw herself at him, smacking him with her bouquet and her free hand. He raised his arms to protect his head, which only made his bride employ her feet to kick his exposed areas.

Naturally, those around the couple surged forward to intervene, but not before the air filled with petals raining back down to earth.

Her anger expended, Lily collapsed into her father's arms, emotionally spent. The spectacle was over.

Believing the situation required someone to take charge, I ushered everyone from the chapel again.

"Let's all head to the banquet room, please," I implored. "The police will want to find the bodies as they are."

Following the last guests out, I shut the door and took a moment to lean against it. All I wanted was a nice, easy wedding. Perfectly planned, perfectly executed ... was that too much to ask? Shoving away from the door while the last guests were still in sight, I didn't want to find myself alone in the castle.

There was a killer here. One who had already claimed two victims. That they were trying to ruin Lily's day was not in question, but what worried me was what they might do next and whether they might perpetrate their next heinous crime before the cops could come to save us.

Dwindling Guest List

Mindy was waiting for me at the ornate banquet room doors.

"Some of the guests are leaving, Auntie. They say they want to get away before the storm hits and that the castle will be uninhabitable in a few hours when the temperature drops."

Of course, with the electricity off there was no heating as well as no lighting. A small generator provided a supply to the castle's central office and a few other vital systems, but did not have the capacity to run either heat or light to such a large building.

Centuries ago, people lived here and thought their surroundings to be palatial, no doubt. Now though, humanity was softer and used to modern comforts. I was firmly in their camp.

"Should we convince them to stay until the police get here?"

I bit my lip. "I don't see how we can do that, Mindy."

"But the killer could be among those who want to leave."

"Agreed. But that's a problem for the police, not us. Besides, if the killer wants to leave, I implore them to go. That way there won't be any more untimely deaths."

"Good point," Mindy conceded. "So, what do we do now? This feels like uncharted territory, despite all the recent wedding disasters."

What do we do now? What a brilliant question. It framed our situation nicely. With the wedding off, our job was done. We could get the catering staff in the kitchen to stop what they were doing, hand some money to the castle manager, and go home.

We could.

But I knew I wouldn't be happy if we did.

Suppressing a sigh, I said, "We get to the bottom of who came here to ruin Lily's wedding. Whoever stabbed Robbie Purcell was in the chapel and that means the killer is one of the guests. Someone would have spotted a person who doesn't belong."

"What about castle staff?" Mindy challenged my thinking. "You always say staff fade into the background and go unnoticed."

"That is what I say." It was one of my mantras, a thing I explained to the people who work for me. Like Victorian kids they should be seen but not heard and go about their business in such a manner that the wedding party and guests never really notice them. "Okay, so we should include the castle staff and look at recently employed people."

"You want me to get Amber and Buster?" Mindy was already moving toward the stairs when she said it, certain of my answer.

I nodded. Buster could employ his nose as well as his ears. It wasn't the most reliable in the canine world, but a heck of a lot better than a human's. He could sniff for blood – surely there would be some transference when the killer stabbed Robbie. He could also sniff the poor dead vicar and weave among the guests in the banquet hall to smell if anyone carried his scent. Twisting the poor man's head off would leave a scent. Then there was Lily's car. Maybe he would find someone smelling of fuel. I could only guess and hope.

The police would be here in another thirty minutes or so. It would be refreshing to identify a potential suspect before they arrived.

Mind attuned to sleuth mode, I made my way into the banquet hall.

"There she is!" barked Aaron Page, one of Lily's friends. He had his phone in his hand and a small crowd around him all doing the same. "She's the one to blame for this."

Taken aback, my feet stalled. How was I to blame?

"The Wedding Doomer. That's what they call her. It's in all the papers!" Aaron came at me, supported and made confident by the dozen or so angry-faced guests backing him up. They were all from Lily's half of the guest list. Naturally, she had friends in the music industry or from the celebrity gossip side of things. She was successful, so those wanting a slice of the action gravitated toward her.

My hand was to my chest, my brain fighting to find a suitable response. Aaron was right in that the papers had recently made a big thing out of my run of failed weddings, but none of them were my fault. I plan flawless days with contingencies in place to ensure minor hurdles never become problematic obstacles. However, I am yet to find a way to mitigate against the bride going missing, or the groom murdering the mother-in-law before the ceremony.

The latter of those is yet to occur, thank goodness, but give it time.

"Why didn't you warn us?" Aaron demanded, his question echoed by those around him. They were all looking down at me, my petite size making life harder once again. "You should have had the decency to pull out of the wedding and let someone else take over."

"Yeah," said Emily Gates, a social media troublemaker with a foul tongue, "this is all your doing, you stupid old bag."

No one enjoys being called names, and I am no exception. For the last couple of months, I have held my tongue, refusing to rise to goading from reporters about the 'Wedding Doomer' title, but there is an end to my tether, and I had just reached it.

My right hand flattened and began to move. I was going to slap the ugly clean off Emily Gates' face.

Justin stepped in front of me.

"Thank you, everyone. There is no need for name calling." He spoke calmly and politely, diffusing the situation just as more people looked our way.

"Here, here," said Lily's father, a rock of sanity in an environment spiralling out of control. "Mrs Philips cannot be held responsible for what has transpired here today. She didn't hurl a brick through a window. Nor did she set fire to my daughter's car."

"But she was the one who went to check on the vicar when the lights went out," Aaron persisted, his point echoed once again by those around him. "How do we know she didn't kill him before he could get the lights back on and then sabotage the fuse box?"

"To what advantage?" I begged him to explain. "You're the one pointing out my reputation is in tatters. I'm struggling to get new clients because gossiping fools want to blame me for the actions of other people. More than anyone, I needed this wedding to proceed without a hitch."

"More than the bride?" sneered Emily.

She had me there and everyone knew it. There was no response I could give that would make my comment seem anything other than selfish.

Mercifully, a kerfuffle by the banquet room's other exit saved me.

"But you cannot leave," argued Kerry Kirby, the castle manager. "The police are on their way and there is a terrible storm approaching. Attempting the high pass to travel home would be foolhardy in the extreme."

He was addressing a glut of people with suitcases. They had changed out of their wedding clothes into outfits more suitable for travel. Among them I could see the groom's family – his brothers and cousins along with his sisters-in-law and their children.

"So what do you propose?" asked Clyde, Dean's oldest brother. "The castle is already growing cold, soon it will be too dark to see anything, and since there is a crazy killer on the loose here, I can assure you I am taking my wife and kids somewhere else."

Kerry looked pained. "Sir, it's just not safe. If you insist on leaving, you will have to take the longer route around the valley. That will take you away from the storm and keep you in the low ground. Have you arranged alternative accommodation? Or are you trying to make it to the motorway so you can get home?"

The nearest motorway was a two-hour drive on a good day. It is beautiful up here in the highlands, but it is remote and when the weather comes down, it means it.

"There is no alternative accommodation. We called every hotel, bed and breakfast, or guest house in a twenty-mile radius. Only one had rooms."

"We could stay there, darling," said Clyde's wife.

Clyde disagreed. "No, dear. The storm won't be as bad as people seem to think. It's just a little rain. If we leave now, we will get out ahead of it and be well on our way home while everyone else is still deciding what to do."

I doubted that would be the case. Home for them meant Kent in the southeast corner of England, an almost six-hundred-mile journey. Even if they didn't stop on the way, it would still be tomorrow before they got there.

Ushering his kids before him, Clyde picked up his suitcases and left the room, those around him following close behind.

Dean called out to stop them. "Hey, guys! You're not going to say goodbye before you leave?"

Clyde placed his suitcases back on the floor and turned to face his brother. He wore an apology on his face.

"Sorry, little brother. I'm sorry things haven't worked out for you this time, but you can rearrange it all and make the next one even better, right? It's not like you can't afford it. We must get going, though. I have to get the kids out of here."

They embraced; bro-hugging, I think the young people call it.

Dean let his eldest brother go with a hearty pat on his back and turned to his next brother, John. Like Clyde, he was here with his wife and kids and had no desire to stick around with a killer on the loose. Dean shook hands and said goodbye to a few more from his side of the guest list. Ready to depart, they had formed a line inside the castle's main entrance.

In the banquet room, more of the wedding guests were talking about leaving. Clyde's thoughts on the castle and confidence he could evade the storm had hit home.

As Clyde grabbed his suitcases to leave, Dean asked, "What was the name of the place that still had rooms?"

Unwilling to delay his departure any longer, Clyde walked backwards when he replied with, "Loch Richmond Hotel and Spa. I looked it up. It's about as plush as it gets. Even nicer than this place. Weirdly, they said they were full until I mentioned I was coming from the wedding here. Then they suddenly had a choice of rooms." Pausing at the door, he added, "If you're quick, you might be able to get their best room."

Then he was gone, the open door revealing the downpour outside.

I heard Oswald say, "We should call them now and reserve some rooms. I don't fancy driving all the way home today, not with the sun already setting, but if the castle is going to get cold tonight ..."

His thoughts sparked conversation around the room.

Moving in for the Kill

E lizabeth Keats watched the wedding guests leaving with unbridled joy. She even allowed herself a small whoop of triumph. Half an hour ago it looked as though the ceremony was about to take place, but clearly it hadn't, and she believed she knew why: the power was out.

In the middle of winter, the sun was due to set soon anyway, but the thick clouds driven by whipping winds as the storm came ever closer blocked out the daylight. Yet there were no lights on inside the castle.

Not anywhere she could see, at least. That had to mean the power was out. Ultimately, Elizabeth didn't care which straw broke the camel's back. The only thing that mattered was the wedding failing.

"Chalk up another disaster for Felicity Philips," she cheered in a singsong voice.

Outside the hide, the rain fell too hard for the ground to absorb, so it covered the earth like a thin puddle with no end. Streams would become rivers and rivers would turn into torrents as the surface water flowed ever onward down through the valleys to the low ground and into the lochs.

After many hours outside, she had grown cold and was glad to be finally moving again. Part one of her plan could not have gone better, but now came the real test. The wedding guests would believe someone had targeted the bride – what other conclusion could they draw? They would assume the target was still in danger, a concern that would make getting away with killing Felicity easy, but one that also meant she would have to be extra careful sneaking in and then around the castle where they were staying.

She had to find the bride and then lure Felicity to her location. Killing her there would guarantee the world believed Felicity Philips died at the hands of the bride's psycho fan. If she had to kill the bride too, then so be it.

Pulling her hood above her head, Elizabeth stepped out of the hunter's hide, the rain drumming on her head deafening her instantly. Humming an off-key rendition of Lily's greatest hit, she aimed her feet at the distant castle.

It was going to be a great day.

True Colours

Mindy reappeared, or rather Buster did with Mindy in tow.

"*I hear Devil Dog is needed*," Buster rasped in his daft, husky superhero voice.

Amber sauntered through the door behind him, her tail held high and twitching with displeasure.

"*Can you never manage without us, Felicity?*" she asked. "*I was having a perfectly nice nap. How am I supposed to have enough energy for my main night time sleep if I don't get to nap during the day?*"

"Amber, today I need your help more than ever and you know perfectly well that you can do things a human cannot."

"*Very good*," she purred, trailing around my legs. "*Pick me up and fuss me while we negotiate*."

I rolled my eyes. "Negotiate? I haven't told you what I need yet."

Amber slumped into my chest when I lifted her from the floor. "*It hardly matters. You will explain it in great and boring detail, but it will be some silly human thing where someone wants to kill someone else for mating with the wrong female. It always boils down to something like that.*" She rolled over onto her back and lifted a paw to touch my face. "*Now, my fee this time ...*"

Buster barked, "*Devil Dog needs no reward. The opportunity to bring light to the darkness, to defeat evil wherever it may dare to lurk, to stand alone against the forces of tyranny and ...*"

"*Oh, do shut up, Buster,*" Amber talked over the top of him, just as he had done to her a moment earlier. "*You were only just saying how you wish superheroes got more bones to chew on.*"

Buster dropped his rump to the ground and lifted his back right leg to scratch his head.

"*Well, a juicy bone wouldn't go amiss, but that's not why I do it. I live in the shadows, so others need not fear them.*"

Ending the discussion as swiftly as I could, I said, "You can both name your demands after you help me, okay? You can provide me with a list if you like."

Amber lifted her head to see if I was serious. "*Really?*"

Buster stopped scratching so suddenly he fell over and had to right himself – not the simplest manoeuvre when your body is the shape of a baked spud.

"*Really?*" he repeated Amber's disbelief.

I huffed out a tired breath. "Yes. Whatever you want provided it is within reason and don't be fooled into thinking that means you can gorge yourself until you are sick, Buster."

"*Awww.*"

"Now then, both of you. There have been two murders. The police are on their way, but I want you to see if you can identify who the killer is before they get here." I explained what they should be looking/smelling for and sent them into the room to mingle.

Mindy watched them go, then asked, "Shall I go speak to the bride? See if she has any idea who could be behind this?"

"Yes, please. I will tackle the groom and his friends."

Dean saw me coming and split away from his friends to speak with me.

"We need to discuss your fee, Mrs Philips. Obviously, I won't be paying the full amount."

I blinked as though he'd just slapped my face.

"One of your friends has been murdered, your wedding ceremony lies in ruins, your bride is in tears, and you wish to discuss my fee?"

Without missing a beat, Dean said, "Yes. Business is business, Mrs Philips, and money is money."

It was Lily who handled almost all the wedding plans and attended the meetings with me. They started more than a year ago, long before all the dramas that have beset my recent events. However, I had met Dean and until now he'd always come across as generous and easy to deal with. Now I was beginning to see him for the ruthless businessman I knew he had to be. His record label was among the biggest in the world, and he sat firmly at the helm.

"I will, of course, cover all your costs and allow you a small profit, but I won't be paying full price for this debacle."

"This debacle, as you choose to call it, is nothing to do with me."

"Is it not?" he showed me an amused smile, like I was being silly. "The Wedding Doomer, isn't that what they call you now? I questioned whether we should drop you and go with someone else, but Lily's head was filled with the fluff you put there. Now she knows better."

I was being insulted and threatened with part payment. If he expected me to take that and walk away, he was very much mistaken.

"Now is not the time to discuss my fee or anything else, Mr Coolidge. Our efforts ought to be on determining the identity of the killer in our midst."

"Ha!" he actually laughed at me. "Think yourself to be a detective now, do you? I'll be leaving that to the police. If you'll excuse me, I think I can hear the bar calling." He lifted his right hand to cup it around his ear. "Yup, that's definitely the bar."

The groom turned away, dismissing me with his body language as he walked across the room, gathering male companions as he went.

I fumed, thinking uncharitable thoughts, but didn't allow myself to focus on such a negative emotion for long. Instead, I zeroed in on Tailor, the man who accused Ossie, and made my way to him.

Justin caught up with me before I could get there.

"Felicity, the kitchen are asking what they should do with the food. Specifically, Chef Marcus is offering to take the salmon and the venison, but he wants it at cost price."

My eyes still on Tailor so I wouldn't lose him in the crowded bar, I said, "That's fine. Anything we can salvage to reduce the bill is for the best." There wouldn't be much we could do to save money, most of it had already been spent, but every little helps. "Are they about to serve the canapes?" I asked the question just as the doors from the kitchen opened into the banquet room and servers spilled out. Each bore a silver tray of ornately arranged morsels.

There being no need to answer, Justin broached another topic.

"Are you planning to leave today?"

I was yet to give it any thought. I didn't fancy being outside in the storm, but staying in the castle as it grew ever colder and colder appealed even less. Add in the unknown killer in our midst ...

"There's a hotel not far from here. I think I passed the signs for it on the way in. The groom's brother said they had rooms, but I expect they will go fast." Chances were that the guests were already calling them to reserve whatever was available. "Justin, can you call Loch Richmond Hotel and Spa for me, please? Book whatever they have."

Justin's phone appeared in his hand. "I'm on it."

I touched his shoulder, expressing my thanks. "I need to talk to a few of the guests, but please let me know if you are successful."

"Wait, what are you going to do?"

"Figure out who is behind this mess and have my niece kick them in the trousers."

Trapped

James Button loomed over Agatha. "Remind me again why they will all come here instead of going somewhere else. I mean, your plan relies on that somewhat, does it not?"

Agatha continued to watch the rain fall, never taking her eyes off the view beyond the window. The Loch Richmond Hotel and Spa was a three-mile drive from Richmond Castle, but less than half a mile as the crow flies. With her binoculars, she could see the ancient architecture, the gargoyles on the roof, and the families now rushing to get into their cars.

However, she could not see enough detail to know who was leaving, though she thought she had picked out Dean's oldest brother leading his family to their Range Rover.

"No, actually, it does not, and we have been through this many times, Buttons."

"It's Button."

"Whatever. They will leave the castle because they believe there is a killer among them and because without power the castle will be dark and cold the moment the sun sets. Some will undoubtedly attempt to leave the area in a bid to drive home, which is why we collapsed the bridge and felled some trees. They will be forced to turn around and try another route. When they realise there is no way to escape, they will come here."

"Or they might go back to the castle," Button argued.

Bored of the discussion, Agatha lowered her binoculars and glared up into his face. Goodness she was ready to witness the shock in his eyes when he realised he was just another pawn in her game.

"If they go back to the castle instead of coming here, the result will be the same. All we need is Dean Coolidge in a space that we can control. Here would be better, but the castle will do if that is how things turn out."

Button narrowed his eyes. "Not just Dean. He is not the only target."

"No," Agatha conceded, returning to her vigil, "You and the others have your own targets. There will be a time to settle all the old scores and it is fast approaching."

The Range Rover pulled away, one of three cars leaving the castle grounds. She watched it battle through the hammering rain, weaving up the long path that led from the castle to what passed for a main road in these parts.

The remote location made the wedding her best shot at getting revenge. Of course, had Dean not chosen to marry Lily, there would be no need for her elaborate plan to extract retribution, yet here they were.

The cars vanished from sight behind some trees, and she lowered her binoculars. The roads were impassable no matter which direction they chose. It was nothing more than a matter of time before the first of the wedding guests arrived at the hotel.

The sound of the phone ringing cut through the still air until it was answered. A woman's voice rang out loud and clear, another who wanted to see Dean

Coolidge dead at her feet. Their reasons were all different, but quite predictable for Agatha who knew them all so very well.

Hearing one side of the conversation, Agatha could tell the wedding guests were beginning to bite. The hotel had room for them all if it came to it, but she was only interested in Dean. There would be bodies besides his before the night was through, but his was the only one she cared about.

Pushing the joyful thoughts to one side, Agatha made her way back to the hotel's reception area. If there were guests coming, it was time to fetch Morag.

Seriously Unpopular

M indy circled the room, listening to those doing the least talking as she passed them with a tray of canapes. She felt clever for seeing the opportunity to mingle without being questioned why she was moving around the room.

Pausing at the bridesmaids, she asked, "Where is Lily?"

Tamara said, "She's powdering her nose. She's not taking this very well, truth be told." Glancing at Chastity, she asked, "Do you think one of us should check on her?"

Chastity nodded and started walking. "I'll do it."

Left alone with Mindy, Tamara took a blini from the tray. "God, I'm starving. Is there anything more substantial?" The blini came topped with half a quail's egg on a blob of garlic mayonnaise. It was anything but filling.

"Sorry, the kitchen has packed up. There's no power." Mindy thought that was really quite obvious.

"Don't they cook with gas?"

"Yes, but there's no light, so they are struggling to see. The health and safety concerns alone are enough to dictate they shut down, but the warming trays won't work without power, a lot of their tools like stick blenders are electric ..."

Tamara held up a hand, accepting defeat, and reached up to grab three more canapes from the tray.

Watching the bridesmaid load them into her mouth, one after the other, Mindy asked, "Does Lily have any idea who it might be?"

Tamara's eyebrows twitched for a second as she decoded the question. "You mean who blew up her car and hurled the brick?"

"And killed two people, yes. I'm sure she has attracted a few crazies with her rise to fame, but do any of them stick out?"

Tamara popped the last blini in her mouth and rubbed her hands together to remove the crumbs. She chewed and held up a finger, begging a few seconds as she tried to clear her mouth.

"Honestly, no. Lily is completely shocked by what has happened. She's never talked to me about having a stalker or receiving hate mail through the post. She's everywhere on the internet, but people just seem to love her."

"Someone clearly doesn't."

Tamara shrugged a shoulder. "I don't know who that could be, and I doubt Lily does either."

The bride chose that moment to reappear, weaving through the crowd and getting stopped along the way by friends and relatives who wanted to check how she was doing.

Watching her with Chastity, Tamara leaned in close to tell Mindy something she didn't want anyone else to hear. "I don't know if you know this, but if someone is after Lily, it's probably because of Dean."

"The groom?"

"He's really unpopular."

A deep frown formed on Mindy's face. "But he's on TV. People cheer when he arrives at events. I've seen it. The show he hosts makes stars of those who win."

"And what of those who don't win? In fact," Tamara challenged Mindy's perception, "what about those who did win? How many past contestants can you name? What are they doing now?"

Mindy's mind reflected inward to engage her memory. "Well, there's Lily ..."

"Name someone else."

Mindy racked her brain. "Ha! That kid from Newcastle. He had some huge hits. George something."

"And where is he now?" Tamara let her question sink in before saying, "There is a lot of wreckage in Dean's wake. I'm led to believe he screws over anyone who gets in his way. If a band or act fails to attract the sales he is looking for, he drops them in a heartbeat. It's how he has made it to the top and I've heard stories about recording contracts where the band end up paying for everything. It negates his risk and ensures he gets paid while the artists get next to nothing. Lily loves him, and I think she is blind to his shortcomings, but Dean Coolidge is about as ruthless as they get. If you are looking for someone who wants to hurt the bride, I would look at the groom because his closet is full of skeletons."

No Help in Sight

"**M**rs Philipsh?"

I was learning, much to my horror, that the groom had more enemies than a dirty politician, when Mr Kirby spoke to get my attention. He was standing right behind me, the people I was talking to all looking over the top of my head now. I swivelled on the balls of my feet to face him.

"Are the police here?" I enquired, hoping that was the reason he'd sought me out. He said perhaps an hour, and it had been almost ninety minutes already.

"Um, not exactly. Is it posshible to have a quiet word?"

He took me to one side, leading me from the room so we would not be overheard.

"The police have been in contact to explain they are having some trouble getting to us."

"How come?"

"Well, there is a bridge they must cross about three miles from here and it has been … um, damaged."

"Damaged? Damaged how?"

"Well, deliberately, would appear to be the case. I'm getting this from the dish-patcher, you understand, not from the officers trying to get to us. I called them when the police failed to arrive. However, it would appear to be the case that someone has sabotaged the bridge."

I felt my jaw drop open.

"The central pier of the bridge is gone, and the centre is already sagging. With all the rainwater that's about to hit it, the bridge might not survive at all."

I tried to process the news as fast as I could. "What about other routes in and out? There must be another way for them to get to us?"

"Yesh, there is," Kerry replied confidently. "However, the next shortest path leads through the woods, but fallen trees block it."

"Let me guess. They got out to investigate and the trees all have chainsaw marks on them because someone cut them down on purpose."

"Not exactly. The report they gave suggests exploshives were used to bring the trees down. It's quite a jumble. With the shtorm raging, they assure me there is no chance to get a crew out to remove them today."

"So, they can't get to us at all?" I wanted to hear him say it. Surely, the police could see our plight and find a way around the problems they faced. It felt like I was trapped in the plot of a terrible horror movie.

"Of course, Mrs Philips."

Good. Why hadn't he led with that?

"Unfortunately, the lasht option requires a trip all the way around the loch to get here. It's the same route I suggested the guests take if they insist on leaving. It is an extra twenty miles along narrow roads, but far safer in a shtorm. I believe the officers are now taking that route, but it will take them three hours, if not longer than that, to get here."

Three hours to do thirty miles? It sounded like rush hour back home except there was no traffic here.

"What about a helicopter?" I felt like I was the only one employing my brain. "Surely a helicopter can fly straight here and doesn't need to worry about dodgy bridges and downed trees."

Kerry gave me an apologetic face. "It could were the pilot not facing hundred mile an hour winds and severe turbulenche as they come down into the valley. It would be suicide to take off, Mrs Philips."

I looked about for something to kick. We were on our own, and that wasn't going to change any time soon.

Thanking Kerry for his help, though I didn't sound very thankful because I wasn't, I made my way into the banquet room. I got suspicious and accusing eyes from Aaron Page and his cohort, but diffused their looks by turning away so my back was to them.

Buster ambled into sight, licking his nose and waggling his funny little stub of a tail.

"*Nothing to report, I'm afraid,*" he declared once he was close enough for me to hear. "*It might be that the criminal just isn't nefarious enough for my keen senses to detect. They are set to nefarious, after all.*"

Humouring him, I said, "Perhaps you could retune them to slightly mad or criminally motivated."

Buster tilted his head to one side, eyeing me as though it was I who had gone mad. "*But I'm Devil Dog,*" he said, as if that were explanation enough. "*The night fears me. I can't go around lowering my standards by capturing the criminally motivated. What kind of message would that send? Devil Dog manifests when there is true evil to defeat. Nothing less will do.*"

I sighed and wondered what I had done to deserve the help I get.

"So you couldn't find anyone who smells of petrol then?"

"*Nope.*"

Amber sauntered out of the crowd, twirling her tail around the lower leg of a handsome young man as she passed him.

"*I couldn't find anything either,*" she reported when I scooped her into my arms. "*Certainly no one who smells of petrol and the only person who smells of blood is the one who touched the body.*"

A frown squashed my face. "How do you know who that is?"

Amber was clinging to my jacket, her head on my shoulder next to my left ear, but she pulled back to look me in the face.

"*I listened to the conversations, Felicity. Isn't that what you sent me to do?*"

"Oh. Yes, I guess I did." I continue to be amazed at how much my animals pick up from the humans around them and worry that all creatures might be as intuitive.

"I must say," she continued, "humans talk about the most boring subjects."

"*What do you want us to do now?*" asked Buster.

"Just give me a moment, please. I think we might be leaving rather soon."

Placing Amber back on the floor, much to her displeasure, I called to get everyone's attention. Seeing that I was struggling to be heard, Justin pulled out a little bell he keeps in a jacket pocket for precisely that use.

I thanked him with a nod. "Thank you for your attention, everyone. I have an update regarding the arrival time of the police." Explaining about the bridge and the trees and how the roads appeared to be deliberately blocked was all it took to empty the banquet hall.

In a heartbeat, in fact, some were moving before I was halfway done with my update, they were racing to get to their rooms. The castle was growing colder, the light outside was dimming fast, and the wedding guests who hadn't left already needed very little encouragement to decide it was time to go.

Suddenly alone, I chose not to hang around either.

Running into Trouble

Justin had secured two rooms at the Loch Richmond Hotel and Spa, however a third was not available, so he and Philippe were going to have to share, as were Mindy and me. It would be fine for one night. In the morning, the storm would have passed and there would be a mass exodus of wedding guests fleeing south back to England.

Following everyone else's lead, I hurried back to my room with Amber in my arms. Buster ran ahead, bounding along the hallways with a level of exuberance only an excited dog can muster. Amber tutted at his display. A cat would never show such unbridled joy.

Our stay at the castle was to be one day less than a week, so my clothes and belongings were distributed to the wardrobe, the drawers of the tallboy, the dressing table, and the bathroom, as one might expect.

My dresses are expensive – one has to look the part – and are transported inside equally expensive suit carriers. When packing, I am quite particular about how my things are arranged. I transport my makeup in a special carrier I picked up years ago in Harrods. Toiletries go into separate bags before being stored inside yet another bag purposely made for the task.

The process of packing usually takes me an hour or more. I skipped all that and used an arm to sweep the surface of the dressing table into my suitcase. Likewise, the items around the sink in the bathroom went in a jumbled mess for the first time ever.

I was a little more careful with my dresses, but reduced my meticulous hour down to under five minutes.

"*What's the great hurry?*" asked Amber, her attention on her right paw, which she was using to wash her face.

I zipped my suitcase closed and looked about to see what I might have missed.

"Well, Amber, aside from there being a killer on the loose, every last guest in this place is leaving and heading to the same hotel on the other side of the lake."

"*I thought it was a loch?*" Buster questioned.

"Same thing, but Scottish."

"*Oh. Is there a monster in it?*"

"No, sorry. That's Loch Ness. That's a different place."

"*Pity. I rather fancy testing out my monster slaying skills.*"

Amber stopped her preening and placed her paw back on the carpet.

"*Buster, if we ignore the fact that the Loch Ness Monster is nothing more than a myth, what precisely do you think you would be able to do against a creature that is a thousand times your size, lives beneath the surface of the water, and has a mouthful of razor-sharp teeth?*"

"*I would headbutt it.*"

78

"*I doubt that would have much impact.*"

"*Ha! That's what you think. My head is as thick as they come.*"

Amber's whiskers twitched in amusement. "*I shall concede your point.*"

"*Besides,*" Buster continued, "*I'm planning to headbutt it in the spuds.*"

"*The spuds?*" Amber's face contorted with a confused frown.

"*Yeah, you know, it's testicles. It might be a thousand times my size, but a direct strike there will put it down just like anything else.*"

Amber lifted her right paw again, inspecting it briefly before resuming her beauty regime with a final remark.

"*Unless it's a girl.*"

Mindy skidded to a halt outside my open door. "Are you ready, Auntie?"

I was ready to escape my pets' conversation. However, looking about and checking quickly under the bed, I convinced myself there was nothing I'd missed and gave Mindy a satisfied nod.

"Yes, shall we?"

The castle's wide hallways overflowed with wedding guests heading for the stairs. There was no elevator, so luggage had to be lugged by hand down to the grand reception and out through the double doors to the carpark beyond.

The castle manager was there with many of the castle staff, offering assistance to get to their cars, attempting to convince them to stay, and reassuring everyone that the castle had blankets and candles aplenty. They could get us through the night, and the storm outside made the journey around the loch fraught with danger.

However, the guests were spooked. I guess a double murder will do that. They wanted to change their location and prayed in so doing they would leave behind whatever terrible plans the killer might have yet up their sleeve.

Seeing me with my bags, Kerry asked, "Can I not change your mind, Felishity? The staff and I are staying put here where it is safe. We will light the fires and cook food the way our great grandparents would have."

He made it sound fun, like it would be an adventure, but I knew I couldn't stay.

"Kerry, I really wish I could, but I have a duty to the bride and groom. I should be with them until the morning, at least." I chose not to explain that I feared the worst was yet to come. Whether Lily was the intended target because she had attracted a crazy fan, or had been chosen to suffer to get back at her intended, didn't matter. I had to ensure she got home safe, for as bad as things were, I knew they could get worse.

I thanked Kerry for his efforts, expressed my disappointment at how it all turned out, and wished him luck with the storm. Inside the old oak doors at the castle's main entrance, a glut of guests waited, the ones at the front blocking the way so no one could leave.

Kerry had the staff making the dash through the rain and wind to get each car and bring it as close as possible. The young man running back inside to collect the next set of keys looked bedraggled despite the waterproofs he wore.

A queue formed behind me, and I turned to find Justin with Philippe joining the back of it.

I left Mindy where she was to speak with him.

"Is everything squared away with the kitchen?" I learned early in my career to arrange my own catering. In fact, I arrange my own pretty much everything, but catering is one area where I will absolutely not compromise. The chef and kitchen staff, along with the produce they were supposed to have served, were subcontracted by me. I knew the firm well and had used them many times in the past.

"They have elected to stay the night and endure the cold. Chef Marcus believes we are taking the danger with us."

His words were like ice water down my spine. Was he right? Were we really running into trouble instead of away from it?

Improvising Murder

From her vantage point less than fifty yards away, Elizabeth Keats watched with horror as car after car left the castle grounds loaded with wedding guests. They were all leaving! That meant Felicity would leave too and her whole plan to snatch the royal wedding for herself would go to ruin.

She had to stop Felicity from leaving. But how?

To disguise her movements, she was staying in a B&B a few miles away and had been hiking into the castle grounds each day. She paid in cash, provided a false name, and pretended to be on a walking holiday. Not that the landlord and landlady seemed to care one bit what she got up to, so long as she was quiet about it.

Her clothes were soaked, the rain beating down with such force that it found ways through her waterproof outer layer. However, the discomfort it brought barely registered such was her focus on events at the castle. It had all been going so well. Setting fire to the bride's car went far easier than she had ever imagined. If ever there was a point at which she thought she might get caught, that was it.

But the threat of a crazy fan wouldn't have driven them from the venue. Or, at least, Elizabeth didn't think it should. A misjudgement on her part since the guests were fleeing the castle like rats from a sinking ship.

She was yet to spot Felicity through her binoculars and hoped that meant she still had time. Perhaps this was in itself an opportunity. In the confusion created as everyone scurried to leave, no one would notice one more person running about. If she could get there now and find her target, maybe she could complete her task early.

Ok, so it wasn't the way she wanted to do things. Worse yet, doing it this way reduced the likelihood people would assume the bride was the target and that poor Felicity just got in the way. But forced to improvise, Elizabeth considered that this might be her only shot.

She knew for a fact that this was Felicity's last engagement before the royal wedding. It really was a case of now or never.

Setting off on a path that skirted the trees and would bring her into the castle on the far side, Elizabeth squeezed her brain to devise a new plan. She needed to get Felicity alone and away from everyone else.

It came to her in a flash. The castle had a public address system. She knew about it from the two weddings she had run there. Both were years ago, but it was bound to still work. Now she had to hope she could access the manager's office where the controls were located.

A call to bring Felicity to her, a quick flash of her knife, and she would vanish back into the storm without a soul ever knowing she was there.

Soaked

O ur turn came to hand over our keys and watch the poor man run back out into the weather outside. The air was filled with moisture; the rain coming so hard the fat drops were exploding into mist upon striking the ground.

I leaned my head down to look into Amber's kitty carrier. Usually, she refuses to travel in it, but today, since it was solid on top, she insisted. She was backed up against the far end, retreating from the likelihood that rain was going to enter the front grate.

"Are you ready, Amber?"

"*No. We should stay here. Going outside in this weather is something only a human would do because they are ridiculous.*"

Buster growled. "*Devil Dog is ready. Devil Dog fears nothing.*"

"Volunteering to take a bath, are you?" I questioned, knowing how much he hated them.

He angled his head upward to check if I was being serious. "*Um ...*"

"There's an inch of water covering the ground, Buster. You are about to get quite wet."

Adopting his Devil Dog voice again, he rasped, "*This is where the ability to fly would come in handy. I need a cape.*"

Amber came to the front of her carrier. "*What do you need a cape for? A cape won't help you fly.*"

"*It's not there to help me fly. Its purpose is to look cool flapping in the air behind me. Also, it hides the rocket pack I would use to fly.*"

Our car appeared in front of the open doors. It was a hire vehicle, our quantity of luggage dictating that neither my convertible Mercedes nor Mindy's Mini would suffice. Also, there was the Scottish winter to consider. It was mild right now, but snow was more usual at this time of year, and I had specified a vehicle with winter tyres. Far cheaper than buying a set for my car when it hardly ever snows in Kent.

Picking up the kitty carrier in my left hand and my suit carrier in my right, I was ready to make a dash for the car once the young man came to collect my suitcase. Mindy was likewise poised when a disembodied voice began talking.

"Felicity Philips, report to the kitchen please where you are needed. That's Felicity Philips to the kitchen."

I twisted around to look back into the castle. The voice had the tone and slightly electronic buzz one gets across a P.A. system. It seemed incongruous that it worked when nothing much else did, but I knew the controls for it were located in Kerry's office, the one room that still had power.

"Ready?" asked the slightly breathless young man as he ran back inside.

Chef Marcus is a calm man not given to raising alarm until things are really dire, so if I was being called to the kitchen, there had to be a problem that couldn't wait. I turned to Mindy.

"You go ahead. Get the car packed and out of the way. We'll hold everyone else up if you wait for me. I'm going to see what the problem is." Placing Amber back on the floor next to my suitcase, I turned to head back into the castle only to find Justin in my way.

"I'll deal with it," he volunteered. "You're all ready to go now. No need to hold you up."

"If you are sure." I didn't really want to hand the task to him, but he is just as capable of making decisions as I am.

"Absolutely. I'm sure it won't be anything I can't handle." He backed away, heading for the kitchen before I could stop him, protest, or even argue.

Sensing movement behind me, I looked that way in time to see Mindy and the young man make a run for it. They had left only Buster and Amber behind.

Buster was off the lead – it would be quicker that way, so taking a breath as though I were about to take a plunge, I clasped Amber's carrier to my side and threw myself into the storm outside. The distance to the hire car was less than five yards, a space I could cover in a couple of seconds. An umbrella would have protected me from all but the water splashing back up from my footsteps, but the wind would have whipped such a device from my hand instantly.

Rain lashed at my face, forcing me to turn my head away. It was unbelievably cold; the fat drops more slush than water. That it might freeze tonight and become snow was a dangerous possibility that felt far more likely now I was out in it.

Mindy scrambled into the driver's seat on the far side, throwing the passenger door open just as I got to it.

The young man slammed the boot closed when I ducked into the car. Buster was right on my heels, but that knowledge served only to warn me what was about to happen.

Holding Amber up and out of the way, I had too little reaction time to prevent Buster from launching himself into the car. Like the fat, furry, potato that he is, he leapt off the rain-soaked ground like a walrus rising from the waves.

"Buster! No!" I tried to get my one free arm in the way to stop him, but he had altogether too much weight and momentum for me to stop.

He landed on my lap just as my backside settled into the seat. Had he been further behind I could have closed the door and leaned around to open the back one. He would have been stuck outside for a few extra seconds, but that would have been vastly superior to how things worked out.

"*Shut the door! Shut the door!*" he barked. "*My tail is getting wet!*"

"Getting wet? Buster, you are soaked!"

He grinned a big doggy grin and panted in my face. "*It is quite rainy out there.*"

There were a few ice crystals on his head where the sleet landed. They melted before my eyes. Unable to see the handle through Buster's body, I flailed around until I caught hold of something I could yank to close the door.

I was hopelessly drenched and muddy to boot. The outfit I had on - one of my favourites for winter weddings - was ruined, and now I had to get the stupid dog off my lap and into the backseat. The car had been close enough to the door that I avoided getting soaked in the dash to it, but now there was water pooling between my legs where it ran off my dog.

Mindy took Buster's collar and dragged/shoved him through the gap between the seats. Looking down at my dress, I released a sigh and told myself it was a small matter when compared with yet another wedding disaster. Could I avoid the royal family hearing about it? Was I already on borrowed time and about to get sacked from the best gig of my life, or was that just my paranoia speaking?

The young man waved for us to move so he could bring the next car up to the doors. Mindy slipped it into gear and pulled away, driving slowly while I clambered through the seats to settle Amber and secure Buster with a seatbelt.

Finally secure in my own seat, if a little damp, I was ready for the journey around the loch to our new destination. The wipers worked at full speed, but even at their maximum they struggled to clear the rain which looked increasingly icy and slushy. A small band of frosty white began to build up where the wipers stopped.

It made me glad to be leaving. With the power out, the castle would be cold and unpleasant even if the staff made a party of it and warmed themselves by the real wood fires. I was more concerned about being trapped by the weather front moving in, but then I remembered that there was someone out there determined enough to fell trees and sabotage a bridge. That same person, or persons, my brain chose to suddenly suggest, had killed two people and I had no idea who they were.

I was quiet in the car, hoping the police would get to us sooner than expected.

Wrong Victim

Elizabeth couldn't believe her eyes. The body lying at her feet wasn't Felicity at all. It was her master of ceremonies. Positioning herself behind the door that led into the corridor that then led to the kitchen if one was coming from the castle's main entrance, she expected Felicity to be the first person through it. Unable to be certain it would be, she had swapped her knife for a shovel she found outside.

Once unconscious, delivering the final blow would be deliciously simple.

Justin Metcalf lay face down with his arms under his body. More than once she'd offered him an uplift in wages to jump ship to work for her, but each time he'd refused without needing to give it a second thought. Maybe she should just kill him now and enjoy getting her revenge.

She lifted the shovel high above her head, but changed her mind before bringing it down on his skull to finish the job. The first blow made enough noise, and she could hear voices echoing through the halls. Getting caught standing over a body was not on her agenda, so with a glance to make sure there was no one coming, Elizabeth grabbed Justin by his feet. He wasn't easy to drag, but with grunts of effort, she pulled his inert form back out through the door and into the rain.

The old coal bunker she spotted on her way in was the perfect place to stash him. He would regain consciousness soon enough, but she could make sure he wouldn't get out and the cold would do the rest. No one would be outside to hear his distressed cries. Not in this weather.

In a jolt of realisation, she remembered to get his phone, a task that required her to hang inside the old, disused coal bunker to fish it from his coat pocket.

Huffing and panting, she manoeuvred him into position and almost gave herself a hernia heaving him in through the hole in the top. The lid slid back into place, and she secured it with a heavy rock. Her hands were half frozen despite the gloves she wore, and she knew her core temperature had to be dropping from the hours spent outside.

She wanted to find Felicity, but the need to warm up took precedence. Back inside the castle, she looked for somewhere warm and dry. Her drenched clothes would prevent her from thawing out if she kept them on.

Agitated at her failures, Elizabeth accepted her situation for what it was. She had missed her chance to kill Felicity, who was undoubtedly now on her way back to England. Thinking positively, it just meant she had to create a new opportunity. Shivering from the cold, she told herself new strategies would be easier to formulate once there was some warmth in her body.

The sound of Justin's phone pinging with an incoming text startled her, and she had to catch her breath before searching her pockets to find where she had put it.

Eyes wide to see the message came from Felicity herself, she read, 'Loch Richmond Hotel and Spa is really nice, and the drive wasn't too bad. Hope you get here soon.'

Despite the uncontrollable shivering, Elizabeth snorted a small laugh and turned her face to heaven. Someone up there was on her side.

Worrying Thoughts

Looking around the hotel's lobby as I waited to check in, I silently remarked to myself on what an excellent venue it would make for a wedding. The views across the loch would be stunning when the sun shone and the building itself, while not as imposing as Richmond Castle, still possessed the sense of age and refinement one only finds in older structures. Wood panelling adorned the walls, the sash windows were tall and wide to let in plenty of light, and everywhere I looked there were small details that provided nothing in the way of function, but everything by way of form.

It was an architect's dream.

Unsurprisingly, given how many of the guests flocked here rather than remain at the castle, I found myself at the back of a queue.

The lady at the reception desk wore a mask in the manner we all got used to during the terrible pandemic a few years ago. It felt out of place to see someone wearing one now, but I wasn't going to question it. She needed help to get the guests in speedily, but the man standing just behind and to her left showed no intention of lending a hand.

Like the woman, a mask obscured the bottom half of his face, but his hair hid most of the upper half too. Unable to see his features, I noted that his hair style failed to match his age. It was as though a man in his late forties had borrowed his teenage son's hair. Not that I claim to be a fashion guru, but a woman doing the same ran the risk people would describe her as mutton dressing up as lamb.

It was strange that he offered no assistance to the ruddy-faced woman who couldn't move fast enough to service the sudden influx of guests. In fact, she looked to be getting a little distressed.

Now that I was watching, it both shocked and annoyed me when people ushered Lily's elderly grandmother to the front of the queue, and he failed to offer to carry her bags. I might have spoken out had the younger guests behind her not volunteered to help with her luggage.

The entrance door opened behind me, a gust of cruelly bitter wind sweeping in with it. It carried icy crystals with it, the almost invisible particles swirling before my face then melting to nothing as they warmed.

Nudged by Mindy, I turned to find it was Lily and Dean, the bride and groom, coming through the door. Poor Lily was still in her wedding dress. The bottom hem, though she was lifting it with her right hand, was filthy from the rain and subsequent mud and her embroidered silk shoes, which cost an eye-watering amount, were likewise nothing more than trash.

To ward off the worst of the cold, a thick winter coat, a man's one from the size and design, enveloped her upper half all the way down to her knees, but she looked cold even so. She was with Dean, though, a pleasing change to their earlier bickering.

Putting a smile on my face, even though there was no positive emotion to power it, I said aloud, "Ladies and gentlemen, the bride and groom."

Everyone in the queue rotated or twisted to look behind them at the handsome couple coming out of the cold. Beyond them, just before the door swung shut, I could see the rain was now almost entirely snow. The temperature continued to drop, the sun had almost completely set, and it was going to freeze tonight. Would the roads be passable in the morning? That remained to be seen, but for now we were here, and I wanted to make the bride and groom feel cherished.

"Please, go ahead of me," I offered, standing to one side. "I insist," I insisted when they looked unsure.

The family ahead of me were the Carters. The father, Alan Carter, was Lily's uncle. His wife pulled her two children back as she made space and ushered Dean and Lily to go ahead of them.

The couple in front of them were friends of Lily's who likewise stepped aside, and it continued until the bride and groom were at the head of the queue and talking to the ruddy-faced woman working there.

Had I not been watching them and wishing I could do anything to improve their situation, I might have missed it, but the man with the silly hair finally moved. Not that he had been acting like a living statue, he'd been looking around and displaying his boredom, which was a strange tactic for someone in the hospitality industry. However, when Lily and Dean arrived at the front of the queue, he visibly stiffened and bowed his head. The motion made it impossible to see any part of his face. Then he took out his phone and sent a text message. Or updated his social media feed ... I guess I had no way to tell what app he was using, but his thumbs flashed across the screen of his device and then it went back into his pocket, and he resumed his silent watch.

I wanted to ask if Mindy had noticed, but she wasn't even looking the right way. I am strict about using our phones when we are working, but the wedding was over and done with prematurely, so it came as no surprise to see her staring at her own device.

"Messaging Eddie?" I enquired to make conversation.

"U-huh. He's lost another cousin this week. He's getting quite jittery about it all."

"Another cousin. How many does that make it now?"

"From his immediate family or from the line of succession?"

"Either."

"Including his brother, who died last year and was either the first or one of the first to go, it makes four from his family, and seventeen from the line of succession in total."

Seventeen. It defied belief. The British royal family had never suffered such a line of untimely and unexpected deaths. Admittedly, some of those claimed by the Almighty were ageing and could be considered due, but others were young. A road accident claimed three, a skiing holiday took another, and his brother was killed by his own hand while wearing a complicated and advanced flying suit that gave him the appearance of a fire-breathing dragon. That story was just bizarre, but the point is that the royals were dropping like flies.

Conspiracy theorists claimed there had to be someone behind it, leading to stories in the news of known antiroyalists hounded in the street, some for things they said years or even decades earlier. Yet, there had been no arrests, and to my knowledge, the police were not looking seriously at anyone or any particular group.

The police weren't, but one detective inspector was. DI Cassie Munroe held the position of detective assigned to Buckingham Palace. To me that sounds like a prestigious position, but she assured me it was anything but and explained it was a punishment post intended to make advancement next to impossible. There was no crime at the palace, so her annual reports could either show that she had done her job, but that ultimately she had made no arrests, or that something terrible had happened and she failed to prevent it. It was a lose, lose situation.

Regardless, she had a theory about the royal deaths and, in particular, Eddie's brother, Nugent. DI Munroe suspected Eddie was behind it. There was some circumstantial evidence to suggest he killed his older brother, but she had nothing concrete. I knew about it because she came to me asking for Mindy's help.

When Lord Edward Chamberlain, fourteenth in line to the throne (thirteenth when his older brother died) met her, they started dating and could now be considered an item. DI Munroe asked her to plant a bug in his room, but that never happened, and she hadn't asked again.

Mindy and I had discussed his likely guilt only once, my niece firmly stomping on the subject and requesting I never raise it again. She was convinced of his innocence, and I was inclined to agree. I thought DI Munroe had it wrong, but the royals continued to fall, albeit the more distant members, not the king's children and grandchildren.

A thought occurring to me, I asked, "What number is Eddie now?"

Mindy looked up from her phone. "Um, fourteenth, I think."

Frowning, I challenged her, "I thought he moved to thirteenth when his brother died?"

"He did. And then twelfth when the queen died, but two babies have been born since then and that pushes him back down the line. It hardly matters, Eddie has no aspiration to be anything more than he is. His family is rich, and the diversification of their investments and holdings is such that the world would have to end for him to feel the pinch."

I fell silent, contemplating a thought that had been bothering me for a long time. If there was, in fact, a person or a group of people behind the recent royal deaths, a master figure orchestrating it all, if you wish, then wouldn't the imminent royal wedding prove to be the perfect venue to escalate their plans?

In four months, Prince Marcus and his bride, a commoner called Nora Morley, would wed at Canterbury Cathedral. The royal family would assemble for the big event along with other royal families, heads of nations, famous people, and celebrities from around the world. I knew every detail of the event because they hired me to be their wedding planner.

The police presence and security at the event would be enormous, making it easy to believe no one would be foolish enough to try anything, but the paranoid voice inside my head wouldn't let it go. How long would it be until they were all together again? Years, for sure. It made me want to bring in outside help I could rely on to keep their eyes and ears and nose to the ground. The kind of person who seems to see and hear everything and who always catches the person behind the crime even if not necessarily before they commit it, which was imperative in this instance.

A person just like Patricia Fisher.

My old friend had involved me recently when she wanted someone who could pull off a billionaire's wedding on board a cruise ship with a handful of days' notice. I couldn't exactly say I had done her a favour since the billionaire in question paid handsomely for my efforts, but if I asked, I believed she would come to my aid to return the favour all the same.

Except I hadn't asked.

Not yet at least.

I didn't want to be an alarmist.

Pondering the quandary, I missed that the queue had moved forward several feet and there were new people coming in behind me. Ushering Buster forward, I moved Amber's kitty carrier and my suitcase before glancing around to see if Justin and Philippe were behind me yet.

They were not, but there had been people in front of them queuing to leave the castle. I felt sure they would be along soon.

Our turn came and the ruddy-faced woman urged me forward with her eyes. I opened my mouth to speak, but the words stalled in my mouth when I saw how haunted her eyes were. Deep emotion welled within to make me question if she was all right. I stopped myself, though, worried her pain might be bereavement. Her husband, perhaps. I knew precisely how that felt.

When I failed to say anything, Mindy supplied our names.

The woman looked down at her screen, found our booking, and began checking us in. I needed to supply a credit card yadda, yadda, yadda. Her words washed over me, heard but not absorbed.

"Has there been an outbreak of some kind?" I questioned. "Is that why the hotel was empty and you're all wearing masks?" I asked not to get an answer to that question, but to see if I might be right about the bereavement and wondered what answer she might give.

"Och, no, love. Nothing so sinister," she replied without looking up. "The hotel was empty because we had a family event overseas. A large gathering with people flying in from all corners of the planet. The masks are just precautionary. We would hate to pass on anything we might have picked up during our travels."

The response explained everything neatly, so why did her answer sound rehearsed to my ears? Would a hotel really shut its doors and take all the staff away at the same time?

"You're all family then?" I fired the question at the tall man with the silly hair. Ask anyone, including me, and they will tell you I am not a sleuth. Not even a little bit, but my senses were screaming there was something wrong with the picture before me.

I wanted to hear the man answer to confirm his accent was the same as hers, but the ruddy-faced woman said, "Aye, a family business. Many generations have worked this place since it was first opened. You're in room two twelve on the second floor." She handed me a key, a real one, attached to a thick rectangle of white plastic displaying the room number.

There were more questions in my head, but I was holding up the queue and the woman was already looking over my head at the people behind me.

I picked up my things and moved out of the way.

The front door opened again, the ground outside now bearing a distinct white hue where the overhead lights illuminated it. Snow fell, swirling in the glimpse of outdoors before the door swung shut once more.

The new arrivals were Aaron Page, Emily Gates, and three of their friends, all of whom gave me a narrow-eyed glare when they saw me looking their way.

I turned away, my sense of unease rising. They were well behind Justin and Philippe in the queue, so where were they?

Justin

"Justin?" Philippe roamed the halls of the castle, calling for his employer's right hand man, but Justin had vanished. Or so it seemed. No one had seen him passing, and he'd already searched the whole of the bottom floor twice.

Each circuit took him back past the front entrance where their bags still sat, abandoned and unloved. Everyone else who was leaving had already left, and he was confident Justin had not chosen to go without him because his car was still in the carpark outside.

Not that it was easy to see now. The sun was gone and only the light covering of snow, which threatened to be a thick covering if it kept up, reflected enough light to make the car visible.

The catering firm Felicity brought in to handle the food for the reception after the ceremony and the all-important wedding breakfast, were all packed up and in the bar enjoying themselves. Castle staff had a roaring fire in the banquet room adjoining the bar and it was the one place in the ancient building that could be called warm.

Actually, it was roasting if one ventured close enough to the flames.

Wishing he was back in there now, Philippe hugged himself and unclenched his jaw so he could call Justin's name again. His teeth chattered instantly.

Irked by how cold he felt, Philippe almost abandoned his search, but concern for his colleague, and a guilty conscience because he really didn't want to keep looking, forced him to venture onward. There had to be places he was yet to explore. There was upstairs for a start, but why would Justin go there?

His room was on the ground floor, and it was one of the first places Philippe checked when Justin failed to return from his errand to the kitchen. Not that he even made it to the kitchen, according to the catering staff. Philippe couldn't think of a reason why they would mess with him, and he'd been with the firm for too long for this to be some kind of twisted hazing event for the new boy.

Nevertheless, when he completed his third circuit and arrived back in the banquet room to warm up and check Justin wasn't somehow there now, he knew he was going to have to ask for help. The castle was simply too big for him to cover by himself, not if he wanted to look in every nook and cranny.

Thankfully, though there were a few mutterings of disgruntlement which Chef Marcus silenced with a single look, the caterers and the castle staff, almost all of whom were now in the banquet hall with the great fire, agreed to help him search.

It wasn't as though Philippe could leave without him. Justin had the keys. And his phone. Philippe wanted to call his boyfriend, and that couldn't happen until he got his phone back. It was most distressing.

Setting off yet again, this time to check the upper floor with one of the castle staff as a partner, he wondered aloud, "Where are you, Justin?"

Time to Deploy the Pets

I tried calling Justin, but got no answer. I tried again and again with the same result. Failing to raise him, I tried Philippe with the same result. Eventually, I left a voicemail message requesting Justin call me when he was able and tried hard not to worry. The weather outside was frightful, but not in the manner of a jolly Christmas song. Had he skidded off the road? Had he plunged into a ravine?

The fatalistic voice in my head conjured all manner of terrible scenarios, each more diabolical and more impossible to survive than the one before.

"He could have just broken down, Auntie," Mindy provided some sorely needed common sense and reasoning.

"But then why isn't he answering his phone?"

She shrugged both shoulders in an exaggerated 'How should I know' way, but gave me an answer, anyway.

"We're in the Scottish Highlands, surrounded by hills that are more like mountains, and the weather is terrible. Phone service is bound to be bad."

Ok. That made perfect sense, but telling myself he probably wasn't dead at the bottom of a gully did little to alleviate my worry. If it wasn't below freezing already, it soon would be, and anyone trapped outside, even in their car, would have to fight to survive.

Mindy was unpacking her essentials, putting toiletries into the bathroom, and setting out an outfit for the evening. Our clothes survived the dash to the car, apart from my lap where Buster landed, but we were dressed for a wedding, and changing into something less formal was an option we both wished to take.

The bed was a super king, which was good since we had to share. I like my niece, but spending the night with her snoring in my ear was not something I would willingly sign up for. I doubted I was her first choice of bed partner either. However, since beggars cannot be choosers, we were both putting up with our circumstances.

I selected a pair of fitted jeans, dark brown ankle boots, and a chunky knitted jumper with a loose fitting rolled neck. Taking them into the bathroom, I locked the door and changed. Holding my dress up to assess it, I decided to give the dry cleaners a chance to test their skills. It was muddy and appeared to be stained, but it was worth a few notes to see if it could be salvaged.

Using the mirror, I fixed my hair, checked my makeup, and rejoined Mindy in the bedroom.

"All yours," I started to say, only to realise my niece had already swapped her outfit for her usual stretchy sportswear. Her makeup was gone, not that she wears or needs much, and was pulling her long brown hair into a simple ponytail behind her head when I came into the room.

"Still nothing from the guys?" she enquired.

I hadn't taken my phone into the bathroom with me, but I would have heard it if a call or text came through. I tapped the screen to check, nevertheless, pursing my lips glumly when it showed a complete blank.

Pocketing the device, I said, "I'm going to ask around. Someone must have seen them leave."

Mindy lifted her right leg, folding it up to touch her buttock where she used one hand to stretch off her quad muscle. It made her look like she was about to go for a run.

"I'll do the same," she said, dropping her right leg and picking up the left. "We can cover twice as much ground that way."

I murmured, "Good plan," and "Thank you," as I went to the door, but found Buster blocking my path.

"*Sounds like you need Devil Dog's help, Felicity.*"

He couldn't aid us by asking questions, but he is good at eavesdropping.

"Okay, Devil Dog," I bent at the waist to ruffle the fur on his head. "Thank you for offering." I turned to look at Amber. She was asleep with her paws tucked under her body in the centre of the bed, a position she assumed mere moments after I freed her from the kitty carrier.

"Amber, I need your help too."

She acted as though she was too asleep to hear my voice.

"Amber, I will make it worth your while."

Still nothing.

Buster went to the side of the bed where he jumped up to place his paws on the duvet. He didn't have the physical capacity to launch himself onto the bed, so contented himself with barking loudly at Amber's ear.

Her eyes flew open in startled shock, but her expression became an annoyed scowl a half second later.

Buster laughed and dropped back to the floor.

"*I call that the super bark,*" he remarked. "*You're lucky it was on my lowest setting. At the highest level I can bark a cat's fur clean off their body.*"

Amber called him a name I wasn't aware she knew. I scooped her into my arms to distract her before she could fill my ears with my further bad language.

"Amber, darling, Felicity needs you to be a cat. I need to figure out where Justin and Philippe have got to, but there is something not quite right about this hotel. Can you please investigate for me?"

Her eyes were narrow with distrust when she looked up at me. "*I expect significant compensation.*"

"You shall have it. I just need you to sneak around like only a cat can."

"*Oh, I'm not talking about that. We'll get to that part in a minute. I want compensation for your continuing insistence that Buster has to live with us.*"

"*You love it,*" Buster chuckled.

"*I most certainly do not!*"

"Amber, darling, time really isn't on our side."

"Then you should make me an offer I cannot refuse."

A minute of tiresome negotiation later, we left our room. Both Buster and Amber were free to go where they wanted with a simple instruction to find the hotel staff and watch/listen to them. I could be way off the mark, but there was something very odd about the entire setup.

The ruddy-faced woman's haunted eyes came back to me. Apart from the man with the silly hair, who did nothing the whole time I watched him, she was the only member of hotel staff we had seen. Where were the rest? The hotel wasn't a huge place, but if it was open there had to be cleaners, porters, cooks, a maintenance person ...

I sent them on their way with a prayer they wouldn't cause any trouble.

Mindy asked, "Do you think the kitchen is open? I'm starving."

Now that she said it, I had to agree. Breakfast was a long time ago and between offensive bricks, exploding cars, and rushed ceremonies, lunch never happened.

"Let's start there," I suggested, telling myself I would think better with some food in my belly.

The other guests would all want food too; the canapes we served were insufficient to keep anyone going for long. With that in mind, we descended the stairs.

The League

In the wine cellar of the hotel, Agatha argued with her league of vengeful villains.

"No. Just get it into your head that we are not here to kill everyone. If you poison the food, you will kill indiscriminately, and that will make us all murderers."

Button got in before anyone else could. "But we are here to murder, Agatha. That is the plan. What's more, I am going to murder those I came here to kill, and neither you nor anyone else is going to stop me."

Agatha tightened the grip on the gun she had in her pocket. She didn't want to use it yet, but if she was given no choice ...

"I'm not saying the guilty ones should escape. I'm not saying that at all."

"Then what are you saying?" demanded Crystal. "Because it sounds like you are telling me I cannot kill Tailor Ramsey and there is no chance he is walking out of this building alive."

"Yeah, and you said we would all take turns with Dean Coolidge," added Nitro. His voice was echoed by his bandmates. "And I want my turn!"

"Look!" Agatha shouted to silence their increasingly loud voices. "I brought you all together because every last one of you has a reason to want Dean and his partners dead. James," she addressed Button by his first name for once, "he swindled you out of your half of the company when he landed the deal that put him on the map."

"Half of all the money he has ever made should be mine."

She turned to the four members of the boy band. "He sucked you dry. Tricked you into signing a contract that let him walk away with all the money. But it wasn't just him, he had partners by then."

"And they all deserve to die," snarled Turbine.

"And they will," Agatha assured him.

Turning to Crystal, she said, "You more than any of us have a grievance that cannot be resolved with monetary compensation."

Crystal said nothing, her lips firmly closed. Everyone already knew her story as part of the 'Me too' movement, but when Tailor got to the papers first, she was branded a liar and a manufacturer of fake news.

Looking around the room, Agatha drew in a slow breath, exhaling it through her nose with her eyes closed before snapping them open again to pierce her league of accomplices with a hard glare.

"You have followed me this far and the people you want to take vengeance against are now here in this hotel just as I said they would be. Tonight, when the lights are out and people are sleeping, we will strike. But we are here to kill those who deserve to die, not everyone who came with them. One of the guests is our inside man, for goodness sake."

Her last point hit home.

Button was staring at the dusty cellar floor when he mumbled, "Yeah, okay." His idea was to lace the food they would soon serve with arsenic. In a high enough dose it would kill within hours and there was little chance medical help would get to them in time, not with the snow descending.

"What about you?" asked Crystal. "Why did you bring us all together? Who is it that you want dead?"

Button snorted a laugh. "You mean you don't know?"

Crystal looked about, checking to see if she was the only one who had no idea why Agatha was so motivated.

Seeing the blank faces around him, Button questioned, "Really? None of you know?"

Agatha's lips were pressed together, her mouth a narrow slit from which no words could escape.

Since she hadn't told him to stay quiet, Button pressed on.

"Lady and gentlemen, they say hell hath no fury like a woman scorned, well meet the original Mrs Coolidge."

Her face an ugly grimace, Agatha spat, "Till death do us part."

Think Like a Cat

When Felicity put her down and walked off, Amber trotted gamely away in a show of willing. Until Buster and the humans were out of sight.

How many of her naps were they going to interrupt today? It was intolerable. Felicity always needed her for something. Didn't the silly woman understand that her needs were of no concern? Her purpose, as a human living with a cat, was to be there at her beck and call to give treats, love, compliments, adoration, and whatever else Amber deemed necessary, night or day.

It was bad enough that she had to suffer Buster and his endless supply of rear end emissions. Now she was expected to go without sleep to yet again help the humans with one of their silly problems. So what if someone was missing? How was that more important than her nap?

She waited until Buster and the humans were far enough away that their footsteps faded to nothing, then wandered back to her room. There she discovered the door was not only shut, but beyond her ability to open.

Getting angry, she sought somewhere warm and out of the way to sleep. Felicity would come looking for her, probably in a panic when she realised she did not know where her beloved cat had gone.

Then she would explain a few home truths.

Filled with righteousness, Amber found the stairs and made her way down. Arriving on the ground floor, her stomach growled. The need for food changed things, but something to eat was usually not that hard to find, even if she had to catch it herself.

The kitchen would be a good place to start, but arriving there, she found an open door to her right. There were stairs beyond it that led down. There wasn't much going on in the kitchen, but she could smell food coming from below.

Not just food, but fish. Prawns unless she was very much mistaken.

Following her nose, she ventured into the basement.

No Staff

"No, Mrs Philips, I didn't see either of them leave. They were ahead of me in the queue waiting to leave when you went out. I remember him leaving to go somewhere else."

"Yes, he went to see someone in the kitchen," I muttered to myself, wishing I had gone myself. I was talking to Oswald Leach, the man who discovered Robbie's body. He knew who Justin and Philippe were but could shed no light on their whereabouts. The same was true for everyone I had spoken to so far.

I found a few more guests in the bar, where they were getting loud about the lack of service.

"Some hotel this is," I heard a man complain as I walked into the room. I couldn't make out who said it, but suspected it was one of Dean's business partners. I identified the voice as belonging to Tailor when he banged his fist on the bar a few times. "Come on! You have hungry and thirsty guests. Does nobody work here?"

"I'm not the only one who noticed then," I said to draw attention my way. When heads turned, I said, "That there are no staff here."

"What do you mean?" asked Tailor.

"Has anyone seen anyone other than the lady in reception who booked us in and the man standing behind her?"

People looked at each other, pulling faces that asked if anyone knew what I was talking about.

Finally, Tailor asked, "What are you trying to say?"

"That I think we need to explore the hotel and find out what is going on."

"Why would anything be going on?" Dean scoffed, coming into the room behind me. He had Lily with him. "I think we've had enough bad luck for one day without letting our imaginations run wild."

Lily wasn't quite so ready to dismiss my concerns. She removed her hand from Dean's elbow and stopped to speak with me while he continued to the bar where he also banged a hand and called for service.

Lily had changed, shedding her wedding dress in favour of something more comfortable. Her choice of little black dress with a sweetheart design matched the other ladies present. The men were largely still in their morning suits for the wedding, though most had ditched their bow ties.

"Felicity, you don't think whoever blew up my car and killed the vicar could have followed us, do you?"

Had it really not occurred to them that the killer could be among the wedding guests? They were all facing forward when the ceremony started, which meant someone in the back row had the chance to sneak out when the power went off. They could have murdered the vicar and returned to their seat without anyone knowing they were ever gone. Except maybe someone did notice their absence!

Robbie!

Robbie was killed because he saw the killer returning!

Why hadn't that occurred to me until now?

To answer Lily, I said, "I think we all need to be vigilant. Furthermore, I think we need to find the hotel manager. If they are desperately short staffed, I want to know why, but it is important that we know so we can lower our expectations."

"The only thing I expect right now is a pint," quipped Dean, dismissing my worries as paltry. To accentuate his thirst, he banged on the bar top again, three rhythmic thumps shaking the woodwork before deciding he was bored of waiting. He lifted the flap to access the bar area and tested a pump to see if it would dispense beer.

Lily said, "Dean, dear, I don't think we should be doing that."

"Why?" he shot back without looking up. "Because it would be rude? How rude is it that they welcome us all in and take our money only to hide from us? I want a drink. Everyone wants a drink. And once I have had a drink, I would like some food."

"But this is the problem," I pointed out. "The bar ought to be open. There should be staff visible around the hotel, and there are not."

As if my words caused them to manifest, two men, one young and one old, appeared in the doorway behind the bar. I figured it led to a storeroom and other behind-the-scenes areas.

"Terribly sorry to keep you waiting," the older man said. "We're a little short staffed today." He delivered his apology with the attached explanation and got straight to work. "Who can we serve first, please?"

Dean pulled out his wallet, withdrew a credit card and dropped it on the bar. "Give everyone what they want and put it on my tab." He made it look like a generous gesture, but he was worth hundreds of millions. A round of drinks would not make much of a dent.

Shouts for beer or wine or gin arose from those seated and the two men working the bar began to serve.

The mood was upbeat, but only for a second.

"What's he doing here?" snapped Tailor, his face a mask of rage. It was aimed at Oswald who was just coming through the doors behind me.

Dean reached out a hand to touch Tailor's shoulder. "Hey, come on now, Tailor. Let's just calm down."

Tailor shrugged the hand away. "You be calm. I want to know what happened to Robbie. The only one near him was Ossie and I'm not buying that he didn't notice the person six inches to his right getting stabbed to death."

Oswald surged forward, a snarl curling his lips. "And I already explained that the lights were out. You were in the back row on the other side of the aisle, Tailor. You could have easily slipped around behind me and killed him."

"Why you ..." Tailor threw a punch that Oswald ducked.

Oswald came up fighting, but Dean moved quickly to get in his way and with others to back him up they kept the men apart.

"Me thinks he doth protest too much!" shouted Oswald. "Why is he so swift to point the finger, eh? Because he wants to divert attention away from himself!"

Tailor bellowed back, "Why? What possible reason could I have for wanting Robbie dead? We've been friends for years?"

"Oh, yeah?" Oswald grinned triumphantly. "What about when he caught you with his girlfriend?"

Silence fell. Tailor had no response. The two men, held apart by the male guests, glared at each other.

"What?" scoffed Oswald. "Didn't think I knew about that? The two of you might have made up, but I was on my first day with the firm when Robbie warned me never to introduce you to any girlfriends I might ever have."

"So we fell out over a woman," Tailor replied. "So what? That's hardly a reason to kill him."

"Isn't it?" Oswald had the upper hand and was pressing hard to make Tailor back down. Appealing to the audience, he said, "Someone killed Robbie and if it wasn't me ..."

Tailor had stopped struggling against the men blocking his path to Oswald, but the latest comment proved too much. With a snarl of anger, he fought to shove his way through. We all heard the punch land, but if Oswald was the intended recipient, Tailor's aim was off.

Dean staggered back a pace, holding his jaw with one hand. It was enough to end the fight.

Tailor muttered an apology to the groom before levelling his eyes at those around him.

"You lot can continue being blind, but I'll not share his company. You've got a killer among you and you're all too stupid to see it." With that, he stormed from the room, passing me in the doorway without a glance in my direction.

Stunned silence ruled for a moment, broken when Oswald approached Dean to apologise.

"I don't know what's got into him, Dean," he said with sincere tones. "I'm sorry you caught a punch intended for me."

Dean rubbed his jaw again, but smiled. "Nothing a stiff whisky won't fix."

Oswald clapped his shoulder and led him to the bar where the two members of hotel staff were waiting to serve.

Looking through the gap between Oswald and Dean, I studied the bartenders for a moment, deciding with a nod to myself that they were related. Father and son was my guess. The younger man looked to be eighteen or nineteen, no older than that, the older man somewhere close to fifty. Both had ears just a little too big for their heads, and long, thin bodies with chests that were almost concave. They wore white shirts above black trousers and a tartan waistcoat with matching bow tie.

Their heads were down, their focus on what they were doing, but observing their movements, I was looking right at the older man when he glanced up. Our eyes met and he looked away quickly, masking his movements by turning to the range of optics behind him.

He looked every bit as haunted as the ruddy-faced woman I met earlier. A few seconds later, he turned back around, the glass he held now filled with a dark liquid from one of the bottles. He flicked a glance in my direction to see if I was still looking, whipping his eyes away the instant they met mine.

He didn't look my way again.

Breaking my train of thought, Lily said, "I'm going to get a drink. I sure need one."

I wanted to speak with the older man behind the bar, but there were too many people around now. I would return in ten minutes when the initial rush dissipated. Between now and then, I had calls to make.

The first was to Justin's phone, the second to Philippe's, neither of whom answered. The third call was to the police. It was the first call I had made to them, the previous ones having been placed by Kerry Kirby at the Castle.

Explaining who I was and what I was calling about so the dispatcher could correctly route my call to someone who could help took longer than I expected. I tried hard not to huff and glare at my watch.

When I finally got through to a Detective Inspector Nash, I learned the officers originally dispatched to the castle were still on route but having significant difficulties negotiating the snow-clad terrain. The storm was still overhead, the wind creating drifts that people all over the region were getting stuck in.

Locals knew to carry shovels to dig themselves out, I was told, but after putting me on hold to check with the officers assigned to our case, his update could only tell me they were making best speed and would be with us just as soon as they could.

He would not commit to even a rough ETA, which I took to mean at least an hour, but they were going to the crime scene first. DI Nash requested we all stay put, as if we were going to attempt to go anywhere and assured me help was on its way. I wanted to express my fear that the killer could be among the wedding party, but worried I would sound paranoid and panicked, I held my tongue.

I thought about returning to the bar where I could have a quick word with the old man, but it dawned on me that I could call Kerry at the castle. I couldn't raise Philippe or Justin, but he was bound to answer.

"Felishity?" his deep highland twang was like caramel melting into my ear. "Are you all shafe and shound now? I must say you missed a great party. I'm just finishing up some work in my office and I will be joining them. Your chef generously volunteered some of the shalmon and beef and has some of his team roashting it on an open fire in the banquet room as we shpeak. Such shircumstances are for making the best from, don't you think?"

I wasted no time answering. "Kerry, did you see my master of ceremonies, Justin, leave the castle?" I didn't need to provide a description, he and Justin had worked closely together for days. "He was with my other assistant, Philippe. That's the very pretty, tall one."

I could almost hear Kerry's frown.

"No, why? Are they not with you?"

"No, Kerry." I fought to stifle a sob of fear. "They haven't shown up here at all. Can you check if they are still at the castle for me, please? Neither one has answered their phone in more than an hour."

"Shtay on the phone. I'm going to the banquet hall now."

I told myself to keep breathing, and that they were almost certainly still there. This would prove to be nothing more than a change of heart on their part. They elected to stay awhile, had a drink to ward off the cold, and that first one led to another, and they had just forgotten their phones. Except Justin is one of the most reliable and predictable people I know. Changing his mind and not bothering to tell me is not something he would ever do.

"Just coming into the banquet hall now, Felishity," Kerry updated me on his progress. "Oh, that'sh odd. There'sh hardly anyone here."

I heard muffled conversation for a few seconds before Kerry's voice came back on the line.

"It would sheem they never left."

"Oh, thank goodness," I put my hand to my heart.

"But I'm being told that'sh because Justin has gone mishing."

"Mishing? Um, I mean missing?"

"Yesh. That's what I am being told. Shomething about being called away to the kitchen, but he didn't show up there and hasn't been seen since."

My heart began to pound in my chest.

Prawns are Better than Humans

Amber found people but did not find the prawns. The scent she followed down into the basement hung on the air but was fading. That told her the prawns had likely been eaten by the greedy, fat humans.

They were coming her way, two of them by the sound of it. She stepped to one side, out of the way behind a floor-standing rack of shelves. She would explore further once they passed. If nothing else, the basement was warm and quiet and it would take Felicity hours to find her, a fitting punishment for letting Buster wake her up.

The humans were bickering over something.

"I don't care what Agatha says, I am not waiting."

Amber looked at the man and woman. The man was tall and gangly, his limbs too long for his body. He had a big belly that pushed the front of his shirt so tight across his skin Amber could see the hair beneath it. He had on a tartan waistcoat, but it was undone, perhaps because it wouldn't stretch around his middle. His hairstyle unlike anything she had ever seen, not that a cat pays much attention to human appearances, but his fringe hung so low over his eyes it had to interfere with his ability to see.

In contrast, the woman was tiny, shorter even than Felicity, and slender all over. Amber wondered if she might weigh less than Buster. Like the man, she wore the uniform of the hotel staff but with a skirt instead of trousers.

Amber's feline brain observed all these features while registering none of them. They were so boring.

The man caught the woman's arm to stop her.

"Crystal, you're going to ruin it for all of us."

"I don't care."

"You will when Agatha finds out."

"No, I won't, Nitro," Crystal spat back. "He robbed me of my dignity, not just once when he attempted to coerce me into his bed, but twice when I outed him and he made the world believe I was the one in the wrong. I am going to kill him and I'm going to do it now before Dean or someone from his team spots one of us. If that happens, we are all going to jail. Is that what you want?"

The woman started moving again, slapping the man's arm away when he tried to stop her. They continued to argue until they were out of earshot.

Amber lifted a paw to lick it, saw the dust coating it and every one of her feet, and moved it away from her mouth in disgust. Maybe hiding from Felicity in the basement wasn't such a great idea.

Regardless, she carried on in the same direction. It still smelled vaguely of prawns and her hunger was only increasing. Sashaying slowly as though she hadn't a care in the world, exactly as it should be for a cat, she thought about what the humans' argument meant.

The woman wanted to kill someone. A man, from the sound of it, which was good because that wasn't Felicity, the only human she cared about. All the same, humans killing other humans had a habit of disturbing her sleep and there had been far too much of that already. Knowing the right thing to do at this juncture was to find Felicity or, dammit, Buster, so she could pass the news, she dismissed the notion in favour of looking for prawns. The heavenly scent increased with each corner she turned.

However, as she came closer to the source of the prawn smell, her ears picked up the sound of a human crying. Goodness how she hated humanity's need to display their emotions so viscerally. She thought about turning back, but her stomach growled again.

With the feline equivalent of a sigh, she turned the next corner where she found a person.

Well, actually she found three. One was a tall, cadaverous looking man with a beak nose and slicked-back hair. Positioned just inside the doorway, his attention was on a woman and what Amber took to be her daughter. The girl was perhaps thirteen or fourteen. There were tears on her cheeks and on her mother's clothes where she held the girl close. They were sitting on the floor in one corner of an empty room.

"What have we here?" the man said when he saw the cat wander in. "Aren't you a beautiful little kitty," he cooed, bending his knees to scoop her from the ground.

Amber batted at his face, unsure she wanted to be manhandled by the ugly man. However, he used his free hand to produce a prawn from a plate on a shelf behind his head.

"Would you like a prawn?" he asked, dangling it just out of reach. Flicking his eyes from Amber to the woman, he repeated his question, "Is she allowed a prawn, Morag?"

"That's not my cat," Morag replied. "I don't like cats."

The man's attention refocused on Amber's face. "Well, in that case ..." he gave her the prawn, a fat, pink juicy thing she crunched and swallowed without ever taking her eyes off the plate behind him.

That he was holding the woman and the girl captive was completely obvious, but it was a problem Amber elected to tackle later. There were prawns to be eaten first. Besides, the woman didn't like cats.

Lies Uncovered

"Auntie, I think I've found something," Mindy announced as she rejoined me. She'd been off on her own quest for information.

"Justin has gone missing," I reported, keen to hear what she had to say, but since we were trying to find our friends, I believed my news took priority.

"You mean back at the castle? Or after he left it?"

"He never left. At least I don't think he did. Philippe is still there. I just talked to him. Remember that call I got to go to the kitchen, and that Justin went so we could get going?"

"Yeah."

"Well, no one has seen him since."

"At least you got through to Philippe. Why wasn't he answering his phone earlier?"

I pulled a guilty face. "I took it off him and gave it to Justin, remember? With the speed at which things happened, Justin never got around to giving it back. Wherever Justin is, that's where Philippe's phone is too."

"Can't they use that to find him?"

"I think that's what they are trying to do, but they are not having any luck so far. I guess the battery might be dead. What was it you wanted to tell me?"

"Oh, um, I found the visitor's book. I think you should see it."

"Okay," I wondered what significance the visitor's book could possibly have. I continued to wonder until we reached the hotel's lobby where Mindy led me to the book and pointed to the most recent entries.

Laid out on an occasional table to the right of the entrance as we were looking at it, the visitor's book, there for guests to comment on their stay, was open at the current page. A duo of pens sat next to it in an ornate holder. The right hand page was blank, the left about half filled with notes in different handwriting. Most were just a couple of lines. One was only two words, 'Great place'.

I began reading them, curious to discover what Mindy believed I should see, and it wasn't until my eyes had skimmed over them all that I saw it.

"These are from two days ago." I turned the page to look at the dates there. They trailed backward in time over the previous week.

"When the lady checked us in, she said they had been closed for a week."

"She lied," I expressed what Mindy was pointing out. "Why would she do that?"

Mindy shrugged, but said, "Maybe we should find her and ask."

Biting my lip and thinking on my feet, I mumbled, "Yes, let's do that." I wanted to speak with the men serving behind the bar more than ever now. It wasn't my imagination. There was something very off about this place. I set off without announcing where I was going, my impulsive movement so unexpected I left Mindy behind.

"Do we stick together this time?" she asked, catching up to walk by my side.

I glanced at her. "Are you carrying a weapon?"

She grinned sheepishly and reached behind her back. "Always, Auntie."

I looked at the nunchucks she now held.

"Yes, we stick together. I want you close by my side when the killer turns up."

"You think whoever it is followed us here?"

"That or they are part of the wedding party. Tailor made a lot of noise about Oswald when he found Robbie had been stabbed. They were right at the back of the church, and it happened when the lights went out."

"But the lights went out because someone smashed the fuse box and strangled the vicar. That rules out the people who were in the church, Auntie."

"Unless we are talking about more than one person. Dean has made a lot of enemies in his rise to fame and fortune. What if one of them met another and they began to plot?"

The moment I said it, the lights in the hallway went out. They came back on instantly and flickered for a few seconds. We heard cries of alarm from the bar area ahead. They died as quickly as they arose, replaced by nervous laughter and then conversation as the power held steady.

Mindy and I were both looking at the lights; our eyes turned to the ceiling when my niece spoke the words in my head.

"I wonder what caused that?"

Paying the Price

There were spare keys for every room in the hotel's reception area. Taking one for his suite, Crystal quietly unlocked Tailor's door. She knew he was travelling alone because the philandering lech never took his wife with him lest she cramp his ability to score with any available women he might happen across.

That was how it happened with her, and he acted as though her compliance was expected. He'd helped to make her. Why wouldn't she wish to slip between the sheets with him to repay his kindness? Well, she didn't, and she hadn't, and less than a month later the record label dropped her. Her promising career nosedived overnight and when she revealed the truth, things only got worse.

It was more than a decade in her past, but still as raw today as it was the day it all happened. Crystal didn't know if closure would come with revenge, but she was willing to give it a try.

The chance that he might recognise her was of little concern, her plan was to strike the moment she saw him, and the knife was ready in her hand when she quietly turned the key. However, upon sneaking a peek around the edge of his door, Crystal heard the gentle splashing of someone in the tub.

For as long as she could remember, her fantasy had been to stab him. She even had a knife bought specifically for the task, yet he would see her coming the moment she stepped into the bathroom. Sensing too much risk, she chose another plan.

Slipping off her shoes, she put the knife away and took the lamp from next to the bed. It wouldn't stretch from there, but there was a socket next to the bathroom door. She plugged it in and only then, on the cusp of getting her revenge, did a smidgeon of doubt enter her mind. There would be no going back once she crashed through the bathroom door. Could she really go through with it?

Crystal answered the question for herself. She slammed the door back against its stop and got to see the shock on Tailor's face in the half second before she threw the lamp. It arced, Tailor's eyes watching it scythe through the air toward the water. He tried to intercept it, but he just wasn't fast enough.

The lights died, flickered and came back to life, a trick Tailor would not be able to copy.

It disappointed her a little that the water didn't boil or hiss from the electrical charge. The only way she could tell it worked was by the contorted face her victim pulled.

Now it was over, Crystal regretted her choice of dispatch method. It ended too quickly, leaving her underwhelmed and dissatisfied.

Using her phone, she took a few snaps as a keepsake.

The power stabilised, but she unplugged the lamp for good measure – like Agatha said, they were only there to kill those they wanted to kill. There was no need to go on a murder spree or leave the bathtub to claim a second victim if the person finding him wasn't wary enough.

With a skip in her step, Crystal let herself out and went to find the rest of the league. Agatha had acted far too bossy for far too long. It was time the others knew they could get their revenge now; they didn't need to wait.

Walking the Righteous Path

Elizabeth parked the snowmobile a hundred yards from the hotel. Once again, despite warming up at the castle, she was frozen. Hiking back to the bed-and-breakfast to rescue her car and then drive it on precarious roads appeared to be her only option if she wanted to finish what she had started, but it was not an option she wanted to take.

She took it as another sign from heaven when she spotted the snowmobile in the garage behind the castle. She, Elizabeth Keats, was the righteous one walking God's path. He wanted her to be the one managing the royal wedding. That was clearer to her now than it had ever been.

The keys were in the snowmobile's ignition and the tank was full. Needing no further prompting, she followed the road around the loch. Now at the hotel, she could kill Felicity and ride away knowing the snow would cover her tracks. No one would ever solve the crime and it made Elizabeth wonder if she might read about it in the papers or see it on the news, a reporter explaining how the police could find no clues.

Leaving her steed out of sight behind a hedge, her legs almost failed her when she tried to stand. Her muscles were so cold they refused to cooperate, but shivering and struggling, she made her way to the hotel where it took all her willpower not to enter through the first door she happened upon.

The likelihood of bumping into Felicity was small, but to pull off the perfect crime, Elizabeth needed to be seen by nobody at all.

Around the back of the hotel, she found a door next to what was clearly the kitchen. She could see people inside preparing food. Staring at one of the men, her feet stopped moving. In spite of the cold numbing her limbs and demanding she get inside, she gawped through the window.

She was looking at Niles Johnson, AKA Turbine, one of the four gorgeous boys who made up a pop group she idolised in her teen years. He was twenty years older now, but there was no mistaking who she was looking at. He still wore the same haircut.

Casting her eyes to his right, she found Nitro, the band's lead singer. How had they fallen so low that they were chefs in a hotel in Scotland?

The wind tugged at her clothing, making her stumble. It was the nudge she needed to get moving again. The snow piled around her feet when the door carved an arc through it. Elizabeth stepped over it and into the blessed warmth. She had made it, and now that she was here, nothing was going to stop her from killing her business rival.

It's a Trap!

By the time Mindy and I reached the bar there was no one at it. Even the two men working behind it were gone. But there was no mystery to solve. The guests were visible in the restaurant area where the barmen were now serving food.

My stomach elected to remind me how empty it was.

Hearing my belly rumble, Mindy said, "Exactly that. I'm starving. Shall we eat first and solve crimes later?"

I was too hungry to argue, and sitting down to eat would guarantee one of the barmen would come over to our table. That could be my opportunity to learn something.

Selecting a table at the edge of the room, a few of the wedding guests looked my way and I got a few nods of greeting. The mood in the room was sombre, their earlier merriment dampened by Tailor's outburst.

Oswald was sitting with Dean, Lily, and two more of Dean's team. They had finished their food and were sitting in silence. People at other tables were chatting but doing so quietly.

Mindy waved to the older of the two male members of staff, needing two attempts to get his attention. He indicated that he was coming but cleared away the plates and cutlery from Dean's table first. Only once he'd returned those through a door that had to lead to the kitchen did he come to us.

"Good evening, ladies, sorry about the wait. I'm afraid we are offering a reduced service tonight. As I'm sure you are aware, we are incredibly short on staff, so we have just two choices of food on offer, steak or chicken, plus a vegetarian option."

That explained why there were no menus on the table.

"Can I start you with a drink?"

"Just water for me, please," said Mindy.

Saying, "Likewise," I moved my hand to reveal a piece of paper hidden beneath it. It faced him so he could see what I had written on it, 'Are you in trouble?'.

I was looking at his face, watching when his eyes flitted over the words. They flared a little and his bottom lip trembled. My stomach tightened. There *was* something going on. Now I needed to find out what it was and who was involved.

I turned the piece of paper over. On the reverse side it read, 'We can help!'.

His eyes flicked up to meet mine, and he gave an almost imperceptible shake of his head. A tear formed in the corner of his left eye.

"What will it be, ladies? I recommend the steak. If you're a fan of beef, there's nothing finer than a locally bred Aberdeen Angus." His deep Scottish brogue wobbled a little, his voice betraying the emotion welling within.

Should I push him? Mindy is a very capable young lady when it comes to over-powering and subduing people, but what if they were armed? Was it better to let it go? The police *were* coming. I could hand the whole mess over to them when they arrived.

Unable to decide what the right course might be and unwilling to make a decision that might make things worse, I said, "The steak, please. Medium rare."

"The same for me," echoed Mindy, "but make mine blue, please. I want it still mooing."

The waiter left us, wending his way back across the room to the kitchen.

Across the room, Dean got to his feet.

"I'm going to fetch Tailor. The man deserves to eat. When I bring him in, I don't want to hear any more talk about Robbie and who murdered him. Okay?" He looked around the room, his eyes daring anyone to argue. When no one did, he leaned down to kiss Lily's cheek and patted Oswald on the shoulder when he passed.

I watched him go.

"Auntie," Mindy drew my attention back to her with a whisper, "he's being forced to do things he doesn't want to do. Whoever is behind that must have his kids or something."

The same thought had occurred to me. My mind flashed back to the ruddy-faced woman who checked us in. Being forced to work under duress with the threat of violence against loved ones would explain the haunted look in her eyes. It also explained the man standing behind her and the total lack of assistance he gave. He hadn't been there for moral support or to lend a hand if needed. His task was to make sure she did as she was told and didn't try to raise the alarm.

Not knowing who we were dealing with or what they might do made any action on our part a risk. Not that I'm suggesting I was thinking in terms of heroic actions, but if I knew for certain that the killer had followed us here, there were enough of us that we could gang together and be safe until the police arrived.

Unless they had guns, which was entirely possible.

I was about to voice my thoughts to Mindy so we could discuss them when a stray thought stopped me.

The killer couldn't have followed us. They had to have arrived first. Somehow, they knew we would abandon the castle ... I drew in a sharp breath when the terrifying possibility of the full picture hit me.

The whole thing was staged! They emptied the hotel of its guests to make sure there was room for the wedding party when they knocked out the power at the castle and killed the vicar.

This was a trap, and we had all walked into it!

Be One with the Darkness

Buster was bored. A gloomy old building miles from anywhere on a stormy night was the perfect setting for him to play hero, but there was nothing happening. When Felicity sent him off on his own, he knew she expected him to eavesdrop on the wedding guests, but listening to people talk was no kind of task for a superhero.

He wanted to find the killer lurking in the shadows. He'd been practising his moves at home for months, perfecting the Devil Dog Barrel Roll of Mayhem and the Devil Dog patented Power Slide of Death. Combined with the Devil Dog Belly Flop Frenzy, perfect for laying out suckers if he could climb high enough to get above them, and the Devil Dog Mega Ram where he could achieve supersonic speeds over a short distance - great for taking out ankles - there was no foe who could stand against him.

All he needed now was a foe to stand against him, and that was where his plan to do something heroic was falling down.

He didn't want anyone to get hurt, but he did want to hear someone screaming in terror. Screaming would justify his decision to run through a wall. Buster considered that there were few more impressive ways to make an entrance than by exploding into a room through a shower of bricks, plaster, and dust.

Thinking that maybe he should circle back to the bar where he might or might not find either Felicity or Mindy, but could definitely do some eavesdropping just in case that would help, he heard someone coming.

He sniffed the air, looking for their scent, but found only the same generic smells he'd been getting all evening.

The footsteps were coming closer. Could it be the killer stalking the halls, looking for their next victim? With that thought in his head, Buster positioned himself in the centre of the hallway, his legs poised, and his muscles bunched, ready to launch himself into action should the situation require it.

Until a voice in the back of his head suggested he become one with the shadows.

Murmuring to himself, he recited, "*An enemy that cannot see you cannot prepare to defeat you.*"

Any second now the person would round the corner and be able to see him. Thankfully, the wide hallways were littered with objects. There were stuffed animals and birds mounted on shelves in glass cages. Tables presented antique items Buster couldn't identify, and a grandfather clock offered an alcove into which he could squeeze.

He backed in, shuffling his backside until he was out of sight.

"*I am one with the darkness,*" he whispered to himself.

The footsteps doubled in volume, announcing the person's arrival in the same hallway. Buster watched, keeping out of sight, but a tickle from the dust he disturbed getting in the gap by the clock made his nose twitch.

The footsteps kept coming.

His nose continued to itch. Convinced he would sneeze if he breathed, Buster held his breath. The person would draw level and pass him in a few seconds. He could hold it that long.

Hoping the feet would give off evil vibes that would dictate his need to attack, Buster watched them go by.

They just looked like feet.

They belonged to a woman wearing black court shoes and thick stockings. A black skirt fell to just above her knees. Buster recognised the outfit. It was the same one the woman on reception wore, but this was a different person.

Watching her walk away, Buster decided it was okay to breathe again. The itching desire to sneeze was gone, so he stepped out from his hiding place, stretching off his back legs where they were starting to cramp.

"Waaachooo!" he sneezed so hard his face hit the carpet. "Waaachooo!" His head was on sideways, and his eyes were screwed tight shut lest they pop from his skull.

The person in the hallway jumped half out of their skin and spun around to stare at him. He could see her through a slit in his eyelids. Cursing his olfactory system, Buster ran the other way. What kind of ninja gave himself away by sneezing?

Idly, he noted the person in the hallway looked vaguely familiar, like he'd met her before somewhere, but he was too busy making himself scarce to give it much thought.

Behind him, Elizabeth Keats watched the dog race around the corner. It took her a moment to realise she had just seen Felicity's dog and by then he had gone. Not that it mattered. It wasn't as though the dog could identify her to the police or warn Felicity she was here.

Dissension in the Ranks

A gatha's rage was apoplectic.

"You just went ahead and did it anyway? You ungrateful, undeserving, cow! I should kill you where you stand, Crystal."

Crystal smirked. "No, you should stop trying to be the boss of everyone and get with the program. I came here to kill Tailor and I have. You and everyone else came here to kill Dean."

"And his partners," said Button.

"And his partners," Crystal repeated.

"Well, only his old partners. The new one, he can survive," Button added.

"Why?" asked Nitro. "Why make an exception for him? Why not just kill the lot?"

"Because he's our inside man," replied Agatha. "He's the one who killed Robbie Purcell. You all heard them talking about it. Fighting about it in the bar."

"Yeah, well don't expect me to thank him for it. I wanted to kill him myself," snarled Sparks.

"Oh, stop trying to talk tough," Button sneered. "You're part of a boy band. A has been boy band. The only thing you've ever killed are the airwaves."

Sparks flew at him only to trip and fall when Agatha stuck out her foot. He sprawled across the floor with everyone in the room staring. Crystal sniggered, but stopped when she heard the gun being cocked.

Agatha took a step back, moving out of easy reach of those nearest her while also bringing them all into her field of fire. The stubby rotary pistol wasn't the deadliest looking gun Crystal had ever seen, but it was pointed right at her heart.

She was about to raise her hands when Agatha moved the gun away from her, training it on Nitro, then Turbine, Button ...

When she had completed the half circle, she said, with calm assuredness, "There will be no more making decisions for yourselves. We do this my way, or I will kill the next person to step out of line." She whipped the gun back to Crystal, moving so fast and so suddenly she made the former popstar squeal in fright. "Do you understand me, Crystal?"

Crystal's hands were over her head, and she had dropped into a half crouch. "Yes! Yes, Agatha. All right! Just don't shoot me."

Agatha lifted the gun away, pointing the muzzle at the ceiling. "I won't shoot anyone if no one gives me reason. We are but a few hours away from the guests retiring for the night. We must all pray nobody thinks to check on Tailor. Once the guests are asleep, we will strike. I want Dean to know why he has to die. I want to hear him beg for mercy. Only then will I let the rest of you take your revenge. I hope we are all clear on the plan."

The Search for Justin

"Philippe, at some point you will have to accept the possibility that he left the castle on foot."

Philippe put his left hand on his hip and wagged the index finger of his right in Chef Marcus's face. "Justin wouldn't do that. He's too ... boring." He had been about to say reliable and predictable, but boring was the right word. "Besides, no one was going out in that rain and now it's snowing. There were two murders here today and the police are struggling to get to us because someone sabotaged a bridge and cut down some trees. Something has happened to Justin, and I am not stopping until I find him."

The searchers were all back in the banquet hall to warm up after roaming the icy cold halls and rooms of the castle for hours.

Chef Marcus held up his hands in surrender. "Okay, Philippe. No one is suggesting we should give up, but we've scoured every single room in this place multiple times now. If he is here, then he is hiding from us."

"He could be outshide," remarked Kerry Kirby.

"That's precisely what I just said to Philippe," Chef Marcus pointed out.

"No, you shaid he might have left. What if he was attacked and the person took his body outshide. The shtorm is passing us now. I can hardly hear the wind at all. I shay we do a shweep of the grounds. Jusht to be sure."

Philippe was all for it, though he could tell those around him were less enthused at braving the snow and cold. No one dared to voice their objection, so the search moved into the castle grounds. With Kerry giving directions, they spread out into a long line. The lucky ones got to stay near the castle where the wind was weaker. Those who were less lucky were out on the periphery, but everyone had to trudge through more than a foot of snow.

With warnings to look out for holes left by moles, and to be sure to investigate any suspicious looking mounds, they set off.

Chef Marcus continued to call Philippe's phone in the vague hope they might hear it ringing and that was how they ended the search less than five minutes after venturing into the cold.

"It'sh coming from the coal bunker!" exclaimed Kerry. He was one of the first to it and took the job of looking inside, even though he feared what he might find. "It'sh him!" he shouted so everyone would hear. They were already coming his way, the line of searchers collapsing in on itself now that the need to be spread out was gone.

When Justin didn't respond to Kerry's voice, he clambered on top of the bunker and reached down to find his head. Feeling around for his neck, it shocked him to find a pulse. Justin's skin was cold like ice, but the man was alive.

He had to climb in with him to haul him out but less than a minute after making the discovery, they were racing across the snow-covered ground to get him back inside.

"To the banquet hall!" Kerry shouted. "We need to get him warm!"

It surprised Philippe to see them stripping Justin of his clothes. They wanted him warm but were getting him naked.

"It's so the heat can penetrate," explained Chef Marcus, a former army chef. "The clothes will act as a barrier to the fire's warmth. This will start the thawing process, not that he's frozen, of course, but we need to get him wrapped up in some blankets with a couple of people."

"Aye," agreed Kerry. "There's nothing like some shared body heat to get the blood pumping again. Best way to beat hypothermia."

Backing away so they could get on with it, Philippe retrieved his phone from Justin's discarded clothing. The battery was nearly dead, but there was enough juice in it for him to call Felicity with the good news.

Cat Slapped

Amber cracked one eyelid and then the other. The belly full of prawns, combined with her lack of quality naps, had made her very sleepy. Add in the man cooing and fussing her, stroking her fur, and worshipping as any human should, it was no wonder she fell into a contented slumber.

However, the man she liked left while she was snoozing, and she awoke to find a different man standing in his spot. The new man had silly hair that covered half his face, yet he was not the previous man with silly hair she passed in the corridor.

This one didn't have any food and seemed less inclined to pick her up to bestow affection. Thirsty, Amber went in search of something to drink. Besides, her plan to get her own back on Felicity for disturbing her naps wasn't working. It had been ages since she wandered off and the silly woman hadn't found her yet. She hadn't even heard Felicity calling her name.

Twitching her tail in annoyance, she set off to find her. Also, she supposed she ought to deliver the news about the family being held hostage in the cellar, even though the woman said she didn't like cats and therefore barely deserved to live at all.

The man watching the woman and her daughter paid Amber no attention when she sauntered out with her tail held high.

Retracing her steps, Amber was thinking about cream and how a bowl of it would be just the right thing when a shadow spoke to her.

Buster watched with disbelief and a little awe when Amber levitated. One moment she was walking past his nose oblivious to his presence, the next she was more than a foot off the floor and somehow twice as big because all her fur was standing on end. She landed, but the next part was just as incredible to watch as the first. Her legs moved so fast they became a blur. For a split second she didn't move, her paws just couldn't find traction. But when they did, she exploded forward like a rocket on take-off.

Buster watched her go. *"All I said was 'Pssst'."*

Running to catch up, he barked to get her attention. She could cover ground many times faster than his best sprint, and would be gone from sight if he didn't give her cause to stop.

"Amber!"

Her heart beating like a drum, she heard Buster call her name twice, but wasn't going to risk stopping until she turned the next corner. Once there, she skidded to a stop, got her breath back, and risked a peek around the edge of the wall.

What she saw made her heart start again, and she was about to turn tail and run when the inky black blob coming her way spoke with a voice she recognised.

"Amber. It's me."

When the black blob opened its mouth, she saw the tongue and lips and spotted the two eyes above them. It wasn't an unspeakable creature from hell come to steal her tail. It was the stupid dog again.

"Buster, why are you black?"

"I am one with the night," he boasted proudly.

"Okay, Buster, I'll rephrase. How are you black?"

"The darkness in my soul ..."

Amber slapped his face with a paw that moved so fast he didn't even see it.

"The spirit of a dead ninja warrior ..."

This time when she hit him, she kept the paw raised, encouraging him with her eyebrows to dare to continue with the nonsense.

Chuckling, Buster said, *"I found an old fireplace. There was lots of soot in it. I rolled around a bit and hey presto, I am one with the night. Cool, isn't it?"*

Amber turned her paw around to find it coated with a layer of fine black particles.

"Ewww!"

Ignoring her protests, but taking pleasure in watching Amber attempt to remove the soot without using her tongue, Buster asked, *"Where have you been?"*

With a fat frown creasing her forehead, Amber tried to rub her paw on the old wooden floorboards and against the wall. Her efforts only drove the soot deeper into her fur.

"I found someone who fed me prawns and then I took a nap. Where have you been?"

Exasperated, Buster said, *"I was doing my job. Looking for the killer."*

Still focused on her paw, Amber mumbled, *"Did you find them?"*

"Nah. I did bump into someone, but … well, this will sound weird, but it was someone I know. I haven't smelled her in a long time, but I'm sure it was someone from home. Like I've seen her in the boutique or something."

"Okay, well that's very interesting, Buster." Amber gave up trying to clean her paw. *"But I need to find Felicity. There is a woman and a child being held hostage in the cellar, and I assume she will want to know about that."*

Buster found himself nodding in agreement. The presence of hostages was an interesting piece of information when Amber's words finally connected in his brain.

"Hostages?"

Amber started walking, heading back toward the stairs that would take her up to the ground floor.

"That's right. They are back that way. Go check for yourself if you don't believe me."

Buster twisted his head to look where they had come from. He'd been idly wandering the hotel, practicing his stealth mode and merging with the shadows when Amber happened along. Playing darkness personified had broken the boredom, but now there was a real task on which he could test his skill.

A hero's task.

He glanced at Amber sauntering away and made his decision. If he was ever going to earn the cloak he coveted, his actions would have to justify it.

Dark Avenger

Buster eased around a corner, checking his six and sniffing for trouble. He couldn't hear anything beyond a few background noises and the gentle moaning of the wind outside. Caught between his desire to rush boldly into whatever situation awaited him and the belief that caution might be his ally, he was making as little noise as possible while moving as swiftly as he dared.

Amber said the hostages were 'back there' but that left a lot of territory to explore, so it was with grateful thanks that he heard a child gently crying and a woman's voice attempting to soothe her.

Convinced he had now found them; he slowed his pace. The voices were growing louder as he drew nearer.

"Hey. No talking." A gruff man's voice demanded.

All doubt obliterated, Buster came to the edge of a door and could smell the humans within. He didn't know if he was dealing with one person or multiple people. He didn't know if they were armed with weapons that could hurt him, but he was going in regardless.

Backing away from the door to give himself a run up, he took a moment to prepare.

"*I am the night,*" he whispered to himself. "*I am the manifestation of darkness. My will is righteous, my voice is justice. I will not fail. I am Devil Dog.*"

Turbine frowned. "Did either of you just hear something?"

"*Dun, dun, DAH!*"

Turbine heard the maniacal barking in the instant before Buster rushed through the doorway. His heart skipped a beat, his brain supplying images of enormous dogs with sharp teeth, and he almost laughed with relief to see the pudgy bulldog career around the doorframe, but his amusement faded sharply when he saw just how fast the dog was going.

Buster hit the man's shins with his forehead, driving them backward almost as though they were not there. Like a garage door folding into the roof, Turbine found himself horizontal, three feet off the floor and watching it come toward his face.

Reversing direction, Buster got his body facing back the way he came just as the man slammed into the ground with a pain-filled, "Ooooff," of air leaving his lungs.

Not finished by a long shot, Buster burst into another sprint, running up the back of the man's legs before leaping as high as he could to crash down between his shoulder blades. If the man had any air left in his body, it left him then, but Buster still wasn't done. Feeling anything but brave, his actions were driven by gut-wrenching terror. If the man got up, he might fight back.

Buster didn't know Turbine was in serious pain from a splintered tibia, a cracked jaw, a dislocated shoulder where he landed with one arm under his body, and severely bruised testicles where Buster stamped on them when running up his back. The man wasn't getting up, but for good measure, Buster bit hold of his head and gave it a shake.

Morag and her daughter were yet to speak. Their mouths hanging open, they were glad to have the menacing guard magically out of the equation but were now attempting to fathom just what had attacked him. Whatever it was wore a cloud of black dust like a shroud around its body. It was as though a shadow had come to life just to enable their rescue.

Penny asked, "Is that a dog, ma?"

Taking her daughter's hand and pulling her to her feet, Morag said, "Yes, dear, I believe it is. Now let's get out of here."

From the corner of his eye, Buster saw the woman and the girl leave, both running from the room without a glance in his direction.

He spat out the man's head, taking a small piece of Turbine's right ear where it was trapped between his teeth. The man squealed in pain but wasn't about to get up.

"*Hey!*" Buster barked, running from the room. "*Hey, wait for me!*"

Two seconds later, he rushed back in. "*Almost forgot!*"

Turbine tensed his battered body, flailing with his one good arm to fend the dog off, but Buster didn't attack. He lifted his back leg and cheered. "*High five!*" before once again racing from the room to follow the ladies.

No Time to Panic

I stiffened when Mindy jumped to her feet. Her nunchucks were out and in her hand before she was fully standing, her eyes like laser beams aimed at the door leading out of the restaurant. Her mouth settled into a thin-lipped grimace that spoke of imminent violence.

Someone was running, their footfalls echoing in the hallway outside as they drew nearer.

The sudden appearance of a weapon in my niece's hand drew multiple gasps, but not nearly so many as when Dean burst back through the door. The top half of his suit was soaked, his tie missing, and there was water dripping from his sleeves when he barrelled into the room.

"Tailor's dead!" he shouted. "I think someone killed him!"

I was halfway through my steak, but all thoughts of finishing it went out of my head. Another murder? Surely not. I felt sick to my stomach.

Cries of disbelief arose amid a barrage of questions, the guests surging to their feet to meet Dean as he staggered the last yards to the nearest table.

"Where?" Oswald begged to know. "Where is he, Dean? Are you sure he's dead?"

Dean was out of breath, drawing in great gulps of air to replenish his body.

Snatching words between gasps, he managed, "In his room. I found him in the bath."

Oswald ran to the doors, Lily's father, and two more of the men chasing after him.

Despite his breathless state, Dean shouted, "No! Don't go out there!" When his words gave them pause, Dean pushed himself upright to explain. "Don't you see? Whoever killed Robbie came with us! Or followed us here!" He looked around the tables, his eyes flitting swiftly from face to face. "Who isn't here? Who among us could have killed Tailor?"

His question caused everyone to look at everyone else. Unvoiced questions filled the room as the wedding guests tried to identify the person who wasn't with them.

"No one," said Lily. "The only person who wasn't here is you, Dean."

I didn't think it was supposed to sound like an accusation, but that's how everyone received it.

Oswald instantly jumped to Dean's defence. "Well Dean didn't kill him!"

"How can we be sure?" asked Lily's grandmother. With a wobbly hand she aimed her walking stick at him. "Why are his arms all wet?"

Dean's face showed his incredulity. "Because I had to haul Tailor from the tub, you daft old bat!"

Acting like she'd been slapped, Lily shouted, "Don't you call my grandmama names!"

Dean bowed his head, regretting his words. "Sorry, darling, but seriously. I found Tailor in the bathtub. His face was under the water, and he wasn't moving. I had to try to revive him. I pulled him out and gave mouth to mouth. Someone killed him and it wasn't me!"

"It wasn't me either," Oswald pointed out. "I haven't left this room since Tailor did." He scanned around the room, pausing here and there to level accusing stares. "So those of you still harbouring a doubt about whether I had anything to do with Robbie's murder ..."

"That's right." Dean moved to his junior partner's side and put an arm around his shoulders. "Now is not the time to be fighting among ourselves. Whoever came after Lily today, whoever torched her car and murdered the vicar, they are in this hotel, and we need to get out of here."

"In the snow?" questioned Lily's grandmother, and she wasn't the only dissenting voice. "You must be crazy. That's a death sentence out there. I think I'll take my chances with a killer."

Lily's father voiced his opinion. "My mother is right. Think about it," he implored the audience, "if we stay here in this room, nothing bad can happen. A lone killer won't strike in the open and not when there are so many of us to fight them off. Tailor was drowned, you say?"

Dean nodded, "That's right."

"And the vicar was strangled, and Robbie was stabbed. That gives us reason to hope the killer doesn't have any firearms. If they show up here with a knife or an axe or ..." he laughed nervously and stole a line from a board game, "a candlestick in the library, then we will overpower whoever it is and neutralise the threat. We know the police are coming. In the next hour or hours, they will find their way through the snow, and this will all be over. Now is not the time for panic."

"He's right," Mindy mumbled, talking around the piece of steak she was munching. Unlike me, the shocking news of yet another murder hadn't put her off her food. She was still standing, the nunchucks looped around the back of her neck so they dangled over her collar bones while she held the steak in one hand and tore pieces off with her teeth.

A lady, my niece is not.

Thankfully, Lily's father had done the trick. Calm was returning.

It didn't last very long.

Rescue, at Last

P hilippe squinted through the window, hope welling as he stared and dared to believe. It was! There were headlights approaching! Just one set, but in this weather, that had to mean the police had finally found a way through.

Away from the banquet room, he was cold, but keeping a vigil was necessary and he was taking his turn.

Watching the headlights creep closer, he waited until he could see the police livery on the side of the car before taking out his phone. The squad car, a Land Rover Discovery, wore a thick coat of snow which clung to the roof, bonnet, and doors. Compacted globs hung from the back of each wheel arch, but the vehicle was built for the task, and they made it through the storm safe and sound.

With his phone, which he fumbled and almost dropped, his fingers were so numb, Philippe sent Felicity a text. That important task complete, he called to let people know the police had arrived and went to the castle's doors. He didn't want to go outside, but once the Land Rover's headlights were aimed in the right direction, he opened it a crack. He waved and waited for the driver to flash his headlights, then slipped back inside to wait for them out of the chilling breeze.

Reunited

We were just getting over the excitement of Dean's revelation and the subsequent decision to all stay put until help arrived, when I caught the sound of claws on the floorboards outside. I knew the sound of my dog when I heard it so colour me surprised when Amber trotted in.

I needed but a second to confirm the sound of running dog paws was still coming from behind her, but my attention was on the cat. Spotting me, Amber ran across the room.

Behind me, someone muttered something about the 'weird cat lady' but I didn't bother to turn my head. Maybe it's an accurate description.

Reaching my feet, Amber jumped onto my lap.

"*Felicity, my paw is dirty,*" Amber complained, lifting it to show me. "*That stupid bulldog of yours covered himself in soot and some rubbed off on me when I swatted his face.*"

"Okay." I took a tissue from my purse. "But why were you swatting his face?"

Amber looked me dead in the eyes. "*Seriously? Like I need a reason? He was being all superheroy and annoying. As usual. And then he decided he had to go save the hostages. That's probably them coming now.*"

I had the tissue halfway to her paw when the voice behind me muttered, "Have you heard the way she talks to her pets? She's as barmy as they get, I tell you."

Ignoring the voice still, I focused on something slightly more important.

"Um, Amber. What hostages?"

Through the door, out of breath and looking like they were being chased by the devil himself, the ruddy-faced woman from reception bounded. At her side was a younger version, the same rounded face and chestnut hair denoting we were seeing a mother and daughter.

Looking shocked to see us all staring her way, the woman stopped running, her eyes darting around until a shout echoed across the room.

"Morag! Penny!"

I twisted in my chair but already knew the shout had come from the elder of the two men serving food and drinks. He was running through the tables, dodging left and weaving right with his son doing the same from a different corner of the restaurant.

The family reunited, all four sobbing and hugging with joyful relief. I had a hunch about how they were being kept apart. Hoisting Amber under my arm, I grabbed Mindy's shoulder and trained my eyes on the swing doors that led to the kitchen. Each door had a porthole window at head height to avoid collisions, but only one had a panicked face gawping through it.

"The kitchen!" I gestured with my head so she would see the same thing. "Quickly!"

Mindy needed no encouragement, and my words gave her permission to do something she is not only good at but appears to thoroughly enjoy – hand out a smack down.

Like a sprinter from the blocks, she exploded into action. Honestly, it was like watching a tightly coiled spring unwind in one motion. There were tables between her and the kitchen door, but Mindy was not of a mind to go around them. She leapt the first in a move any parkour runner would be proud to display, somersaulted over the next, and hit the swing door on the left so hard it flew off its hinges and vanished from sight.

The voice behind me said, "Where the heck did she find her?"

Buster appeared at my feet. He was puffing and panting from the effort of running through the hotel and he was black. Not completely black though I suspected he might once have been. A trail of soot showed his passage across the restaurant, the black dust shaking out of his coat to reveal a vague outline of the white and tan beneath.

"*I was darkness personified,*" he huffed, sounding about ready to collapse. "*Devil Dog triumphed over evil to rescue two humans.*"

I wanted to give him a pat, but there was no chance I was touching his fur. Verbal praise would have to do.

"Buster, you are the most wonderful, incredible, and courageous dog I have ever heard about. When we get home, I am going to buy you a steak."

"*Hold on a minute,*" Amber protested. "*I'm the one who found them, thank you very much. Why is the fat doofus getting steak?*"

"*Did you save them?*" Buster asked. "*Or did you decide to eat all the food and have a nice little nap?*"

I cocked an eyebrow at my cat.

Licking her paw dismissively, Amber said, "*The woman said she doesn't like cats.*"

The family were back together, but their tearful reunion had everyone in the room on their feet. No one had the faintest clue what was happening, me included. However, when Mindy came back through the ruined swing doors, she brought a man with her. She had his right arm twisted so high behind his back he was forced to walk on his tippytoes and seeing him a few things dropped into place.

Some of the men, including Oswald, had chased after Mindy, their poor machismo too fragile to handle being outdone by a teenage woman. They were around her now, though they recognised she needed no help and were offering none.

The man dangling in my niece's grip had the same daft hairstyle as the one I witnessed standing behind the woman in reception when we checked in. Of course, now I realised he had been standing guard, there as an imposing physical reminder that she couldn't reveal the truth to anyone.

"Dear Lord!" exclaimed Dean, walking toward Mindy's captive with stuttering steps. "Milford? Milford Jones? What are you doing here?"

Milford looked up, flicking his head to get the hair out of his eyes so he could scowl at Dean when he spat, "Getting my revenge!"

The name, 'Milford Jones,' rebounded around the room in whispers and gasps. It sounded like most of those assembled knew precisely who he was.

"Revenge?" Dean echoed. "What are you talking about, Milford?"

"My name is Sparks!"

Dean shook his head a little, not arguing, but not agreeing either. "Sparks was just a stage name to go with the group's persona. It worked for a while."

Spittal flying from his lips, Milford screamed, "It would have worked forever! All we needed was your support, but you bled us dry and tossed away the husks. We were just a money-making machine to you!"

Morag, I could identify the ruddy-faced woman by name now that her husband had shouted it, let her family go to charge at Mindy.

"Let him go so I can kill him!" she raved. There were tears and snot on her face, and I think she might have throttled the silly-haired hostage taker had Mindy not turned him away and brandished her nunchucks to ward the angry woman off.

"I can't do that," she replied calmly. "But I think it is time we found out what is going on." Mindy hooked a chair with a foot, kicked it so it slid across the floor and dropped Milford into it before it stopped moving. Spearing Dean with a look that suggested she was not in a mood for games, Mindy asked, "Want to go first?"

Revealed

"**I**'ll go first," snarled Morag, her hands clenching into fists that were balled by her sides. Her husband took their two kids to a table where they could sit. "This one arrived two days ago along with the rest of his boy band friends, some insane pop pixie, a man who looks like he died five years ago ..."

Dean choked, "James Button!"

"Yes," Morag confirmed. "They all call him Buttons and it drives him mad. And the whole lot of them are being led by a demented pint-sized maniac who probably plans to kill them all when the job is done. I'm certain she planned to kill us."

Unable to help myself, I asked, "What job?"

Morag flicked her eyes at Dean. "Killing him. Well, him and his partners. I don't know what you did to upset them, but they hate you with more passion than I have ever seen."

Milford, or Sparks, depending on who you asked, attempted to rise only to have Mindy grip his shoulder to hold him in place. To accentuate the point, she tapped his right cheek with the side of her nunchucks. Not to hurt him, just to remind him they were there.

Lily's father removed his tie, motioning for others to do the same. They had one of the guilty people, and the only safe thing to do was tie him to the chair.

Settling back into his chair, though no less incensed, Milford growled, "He knows exactly what he did. The others were guilty, but he was the instigator. Dean tricked us into signing those awful contracts."

"I never tricked anyone into doing anything. They were standard industry contracts. If you had done better, and worked harder, you would have made more money."

There was a look of confusion plastered across Lily's face. "Wait, what happened?" The question wasn't aimed at Dean, but at Milford. "What did Dean and his partners do?"

At the mention of his partners, I looked for Oswald. Robbie and Tailor were already dead, but the firm's youngest partner had made it through unscathed so far. However, when my eyes found him, he was at the back of the crowd, as far away from the action as he could get without attempting to leave the room.

I heard Dean say, "We didn't do anything, darling. Don't listen to this fool's lies."

Concentrating on what Oswald was doing, their voices faded into the background. I could still hear Milford speaking, regaling his audience with tales about Dean. It sounded like the music mogul was an absolute heel, the kind of talent manager that promises the world and delivers the opposite.

Lily had to tell Dean to stop talking, raising her voice the second time to force the point. It registered in my head, but my focus was on Oswald. Too engrossed in what he was doing, he hadn't noticed my approach.

In one swift motion, I snatched the phone from his hands.

"Hey! Give me that!" he roared, chasing after me, but I knew that he would and was already putting people between us.

Leaning around him before I took the phone out of his hand, I could read the general content of his text, but darting and ducking to stay a pace ahead of him, I was able to read the rest.

"He's one of them!" I declared, shouting to make sure everyone heard. Of course, they were all listening already because Oswald was chasing me and making a lot of noise about the fact that I had his phone. "He's letting them know they have been discovered!"

Oswald finally caught up with me, grabbing my arm in a death grip, but he didn't get the phone.

Mindy was coming, storming across the room, but it was to Lily's father that I threw the phone.

"Read it!" I shouted. Oswald was still trying to reel me in, but people were coming to my rescue, manhandling him, and womanhandling him in a couple of instances. By the time Mindy got to me, Oswald had surrendered, and we were all listening to Lily's father read the text.

"Morag and Penny have just appeared in the restaurant! The secret is out, and the wedding planner's niece has just collared Sparks. The idiot keeps looking at me, so I'm leaving before they figure out I'm the ringer!"

It was a full confession. Unfortunately, he'd already sent it.

Dean, out from under the spotlight for a moment, had his mouth open and his hands clasping either side of his head.

"It was you? You killed Robbie?"

Oswald argued with himself for a second, looking at me as though he was trying to figure out whether to try bluffing his way out. Ultimately, he accepted there was no way to reverse his position, no lie he could tell that might explain the text.

Glaring at Dean, he snarled, "Of course I did! I would have been in line to kill you too if I got the chance."

Mindy motioned for Oswald to sit, the hardness in her eyes enough to make him comply. There were one or two men still wearing ties, but not for long. Like Milford, it was safer for us if he was bound to a chair and immobilised.

While that happened, the conversation continued.

Dean couldn't believe what he was hearing. "Why? I've given you everything. I took you from nothing."

"You made me your dogsbody. I run around doing all your dirty work and clearing up your messes. I should be a full partner in the firm, not the poor relation allowed to eat at the same table but never treated as an equal."

"This is about money?" Dean gawped. "You killed Robbie because you want a bigger share?"

"Not a bigger share, Dean. Half. I want half!"

Lily threw her hands up and said, "Wait! If he killed Robbie and he was here when Tailor was killed. Who killed Tailor?"

Dean murmured, "Crystal Meth." Meeting Oswald's eyes, he asked, "It was Crystal Meth, wasn't it?"

Crystal Meth was a name I knew. She had a couple of chart hits in the late nineties, but what happened to her after that I couldn't say.

Dean twisted to look at Morag. "You described an insane pop pixie. That's Crystal Meth to a T, and she accused Tailor of sexual harassment."

Lily's jaw dropped. "Did he do it?"

Dean shrugged, refusing to meet Lily's eyes when he mumbled, "Might have."

Lily was aghast. "He might have? He might have sexually harassed a woman while in a position of power over her and you continued to work with him?"

"Nothing was ever proven."

"It rarely is!" she screeched. "Was hers the only accusation?"

"No, it wasn't," said Oswald. "Dean and his pals have swindled, cheated, and lied their way to the top. Trampling over everyone and everything in their path. James Button tried to put the reins on Dean, and he ruined him for it. That's why he is part of our league."

Mindy blinked. "I'm sorry? Your what?"

Oswald's cheeks coloured. "Um, our league. We formed a league of revenge to bring justice to Dean, Robbie, and Tailor."

"By murdering them," I pointed out. "And a vicar. Was Reverend Hector somehow benefitting from the record label's ill-gotten profits?" Oswald opened his mouth to speak, and I made an angry 'Zip-it!' sound to stop him. "You weren't after justice even if the others were in some weird, twisted, aggrieved way. You just admitted you wanted to take half the firm."

He opened his mouth once more, but a warning look from me was all it took to shut him up this time. I'd heard enough from him. Now I wanted to hear from Morag.

Offering her kindly eyes, I asked, "Morag, how many of them are there? I would ask one of these two idiots, but I don't trust them to give an honest answer."

Morag was back with her family, all four of them standing closer than decorum would allow strangers, but a range that was perfect for a family needing the comfort only loved ones can give by being near.

"There are seven. The four band members with their silly hair …"

Spark flicked his head to get the fringe out of his eyes and sounded genuinely wounded when he said, "Hey!"

As though he hadn't spoken, Morag said, "Then there is Button, Crystal, and their leader, Agatha."

Dean blurted, "What? Agatha? This is Agatha's doing?"

Looking as uninformed as I felt, Mindy asked, "Who's Agatha?"

"My psycho ex-wife." Dean had his head back in his hands.

"Let me guess," said Lily. "You screwed her out of half of the business when you divorced her."

Dean lifted his eyes to meet hers and we all got to see the guilt they contained.

Morag said, "Well, he got the psycho part right. Out of all of them, she's the one who scares me the most. She's the one who had me send all the staff home and eject all the guests. They showed up dressed as health inspectors with clip boards and electronic tablets, and matching uniforms. They looked legitimate and demanded to test the kitchen claiming two guests who stayed here last week were dead. It was obviously all fake, though we didn't know it at the time, but their tests showed high concentrations of salmonella. According to them, it was everywhere. Only once the staff and guests were out did they drop the act and produce weapons. We've been held in the cellar ever since, one or two of us taken out to do necessary tasks such as turn away new guests arriving while the rest of my family," her voice broke a little at that point, "were held under the threat of death. Agatha insisted they would let us go when they had done what they had come to do, but I never believed her."

Morag was an astute woman, and it gave me great pleasure to have them safe now. But how safe were we? Two of the seven were in our custody, but that left another five at large on the premises.

We were far from out of trouble yet.

A Perfect Plan Gone Awry

Elizabeth stalked the hotel. Twenty minutes was how much time she lost trying to thaw out after the snowmobile ride. It was time she didn't wish to sacrifice, but she also recognised there was nothing she could do to speed the process up.

Once feeling returned to her fingers and toes, she ventured a little farther into the hotel. It was strangely empty, with no sign of staff anywhere, including the lobby where she found the reception desk. In a room behind it, she found what she took to be a uniform the staff would wear. The black skirt and tartan waistcoat didn't exactly go with her polo neck top and boots, but she figured it would be good enough that anyone catching a brief glimpse would assume they were seeing a member of the hotel staff. Anyone looking for longer would notice the incongruities and if they saw her face ... well, she was determined to deal with that when the problem arose.

She was not getting caught. Not when she was so close to getting everything she wanted.

Using the computer on the reception desk, while constantly peering around convinced the hotel manager or concierge would appear at any second, she found

Felicity's room assignment. Then, with a smile on her face, and the knife she bought specifically to kill Felicity tucked up one sleeve, she set off to find it.

This part was not only going to be easy, but would be the culmination of weeks of planning. It was the point at which she'd been aiming, and she could not wait to see the look of shocked horror on Felicity's face when she realised she was finally getting what she had always deserved.

Elizabeth would knock on the door, wait for Felicity to answer, and plunge the knife into her chest the moment she exposed herself. A hand over her mouth to stifle the scream and it would all be over.

Except Felicity wasn't in her room, and Elizabeth cursed her lack of vision. It was early evening, and they were in a hotel. She saw no sign of the staff because they were all in the bar or restaurant catering to the guests who were undoubtedly sitting down for dinner.

She couldn't go there, but Felicity would return to her room and retire for the night, so Elizabeth told herself to be patient and looked for somewhere good to hide. A storeroom or office out of the way, or a bedroom that wasn't currently in use would do the trick.

But there were no unassigned rooms. Not one, which shouldn't have come as a great surprise, for though the hotel was beautiful, it was not big.

So she stalked the halls looking for a place to lie low for a couple of hours and that was how she came to run into Button.

He was running when he almost collided with her coming out of the wine cellar. It was his turn to watch the hostages again, which he didn't mind. It was easy and necessary, and he liked being around all the fine wine. They were nearly done, and he'd spotted a 1974 Merlot he rather fancied sampling as a sort of early celebration.

However, when he walked in, he found Turbine on the floor and the hostages gone. The ladies had overpowered him, beaten him quite badly in the process, and for some inexplicable reason, had urinated on his head for good measure. Turbine's broken jaw meant he could only manage an unintelligible mumble. Button could see his accomplice had been hurt, but it was of little concern.

With the hostages free, they could warn the guests and if they did that the whole gig was up.

Racing to take the news to Agatha, he burst through the door from the cellar only to find himself face to face with a member of staff they had somehow missed.

The woman stared at him with shocked eyes, and in the heartbeat between nearly knocking her over and reaching out to grab her, his brain noted that she didn't look like staff at all. Her shoes were wrong as was her shirt.

He swung an arm at her all the same, meaning to snag her collar, but she ducked back out of his reach.

Elizabeth, startled by the man's unexpected and sudden appearance, mistook his cadaverous looks for that of a zombie and, reacting in terror, pulled the knife from her sleeve to defend herself when he tried to grab her head.

Button looked down at the handle protruding from his chest. He knew withdrawing it would be worse than leaving it in, he'd seen something about it on TV. However, the damage to his heart was so complete it made no difference, and it stopped beating before he could raise his hands to it.

Elizabeth watched in abject horror when the already dead looking man slumped to his knees, looked up at her face, and toppled gracefully to one side.

Contingency Plan

"It's over Agatha!" Nitro backed away from her. "They know everything. They have Sparks and your inside man. Some ringer he turned out to be."

Diesel agreed. "If we go now, we can get some distance between us and the police. Maybe get to an airport and get out of the country."

"Yeah," said Crystal, "Like fly to one of those countries with no extradition treaty."

All three had read the text from Oswald because Agatha had foolishly left her phone on a table where anyone could see a message when it popped onto the screen.

Listening to her accomplices' inane babble, it was clear to Agatha that not one of them had the brain to have thought beyond this point. They assumed the plan would run like clockwork, they would take their victims and vanish into the night. In their wake, the trail of corpses and bewildered wedding guests would have no idea what happened or how.

That it could all go wrong had never been far from Agatha's mind, but then she always intended to be the only one of the league who left the hotel. Their deaths would be swift, their bodies arranged to make it look as though they had all betrayed one another and died in a glorious battle to survive.

Killing them wouldn't plague her conscious. Except perhaps in the case of Buttons. She'd developed a soft spot for her ex-husband's original partner. He was the only one with a shred of decency, a man who lived by a moral code that ultimately led to his downfall when Dean couldn't abide by James's desire to do that which was right, rather than that which made them the most money.

Nevertheless, it was safer for her if he was dead. Loose ends would keep her awake at night.

Taking out her gun, she shot Nitro, Diesel, and Crystal in turn; one, two, three. None of them saw it coming, and she walked from the room before the last of them crumpled to the carpet.

The guests knew, so it was time to employ extreme strategies. Agatha had a few in her head to combat certain predictable scenarios. This was about as sideways as things could go, and there was now a very distinct chance she was going to get caught. However, with that in mind, her determination to take revenge on Dean took precedence over everything else.

They were entering the final stage.

Human Behaviour

Dean said, "Look, all we have to do is wait in here until the police come, right?" He looked my way. "That's what your man said, isn't it? The police are on their way."

I nodded. After the back-and-forth interrogation of Oswald and Milford, it had dawned on me to check my phone. The battery was running low, and my charger was in the room to which I was not about to return. Taking it from my handbag, I saw multiple missed calls and two text messages from Philippe.

Justin was alive. That was the crux of the first message. It was the first piece of good news all day and I was so happy to get it my legs went wobbly.

Seeing me, Mindy rushed over, and we huddled together to call Philippe for an update. His texts let us know the police were at the castle, but I wanted more detail. Never lost for words, Philippe filled us in on where and how they found Justin and that he was getting his colour back. The police, two constables and a detective, checked the two bodies as swiftly as they could, and having confirmed the danger was very probably now at our location, had pushed on through the snow to get to us. Their hopeful ETA was an hour after leaving the castle, which was fifteen minutes before I called.

All in all we had reason to feel like the worst was over and salvation was right around the corner.

To give a verbal answer to Dean's question, I said, "Yes, they should be here in less than an hour."

Dean smiled. "There you are then. We can get a drink at the bar. I'm sure Morag and Ian won't mind us helping ourselves while we all wait for the cavalry to arrive. They can deal with my ex-wife and her murdering minions."

"What if they are armed?" asked Lily's father, a question that didn't seem to have occurred to anyone else, but from the looks on the faces around me, was now at the forefront of their minds. "Oswald sent his text, so they know the game is up. You plan to just sit here, but what if they decide to change tactics and attack us?"

"They only want you, Mr Coolidge."

All heads turned to find Lily's elderly grandmother aiming her walking stick Dean's way.

"The rest of us are of no interest. We didn't swindle our way to a fortune using the currency of other people's hard work. That was you. We could just push you out the door and close it. That would guarantee our safety."

It was a terrible thing to suggest, and I felt for sure her opinion would be shouted down, but in a crazy 'Lord of the Flies' reflection, her voice got the majority vote.

"Yeah," agreed one of the younger male members of Lily's family. "He's the one they want. Let's just hand him over."

"Now wait a minute!" Dean could see the tide of opinion turning against him and was rightfully worried about his safety.

I thought I was going to have to say something to intervene, but there were sane voices arguing on Dean's behalf. Not because they thought any better of him, but because handing him over to be murdered wasn't something people should endorse.

Morag's voice cut through the din, "We can escape to my neighbour's house. They have shotguns and I know they will take us in." Heads swivelled to look her way. "It's more than a mile, but I would rather trudge through the snow and put the crazy people behind me than wait to see what they will do next."

Her suggestion sparked a new argument with some of the guests thinking it was a good idea and others pointing out the sub-zero temperatures and many inches of snow they would have to get through. None of them had boots or clothing designed to protect against such elements.

"We could all die from exposure," argued Lily's father. "Do you really think my mother would survive or even has the physical capacity to march more than a mile through deep snow. She's ninety-two!"

His thoughts were shared by many of the older guests, and by most of the women. The latter were largely still in heels and dresses for the wedding.

Others offered to help carry Lily's grandmother, and tried to say that getting a bit cold was far better than being shot.

"It's really not that far," Morag tried to tell them, her voice drowned out by the bickering.

While the families argued, I asked Morag, "Which direction is it when we get outside? Left or right on the main road?" I figured it had to be right because we hadn't passed it on the way from the castle, but I was wrong.

"Och, it's neither, dearie. To get there we have to go through the woods behind us. There is a path to follow and I'm going whether anyone else does or not."

Her reply was overheard, Lily's father shouting, "Did you hear that, everyone. This neighbour isn't even on the road. She's expecting us to navigate through woodland in the dark. How many want to try that and risk losing their way? I'm not going anywhere."

Until the last few minutes, I held Lily's father in high regard. It amazed me how quickly humans would turn on one another with the slightest bit of pressure.

Turning to face Dean, Lily's father said, "Let's just throw him out of the restaurant and close the doors. If the crazy killers want him, they can have him."

Dean backed away, and Mindy stepped forward to stop anyone who tried to grab him. I placed a hand on her arm. Not to stop her opposing the lynch mob, but because there was something far more pressing to address.

"Can anyone else smell burning?"

Between a Fire and a Cold Place

N o sooner had the words left my mouth than the first tendrils of smoke snaked their way through the ruined kitchen door Mindy knocked from its hinges.

Panic spread through the assembled guests like a wave. The building was on fire. Sacrificing Dean suddenly vanished from the list of topics being discussed.

"Fire extinguishers!" yelled Lily's father. "Everybody look for fire extinguishers! We need to fight the fire before it takes hold!"

Dean was the first to respond. "Hey, no way, man! That's a trap. They'll be waiting for us. If we try to fight the fire, it will be the last thing we do."

Lily's grandmother said, "They won't be waiting for us. They'll be waiting for you."

Mindy leaned in close to whisper, "They must have gone around opening the fire doors to make sure it spreads."

She was almost certainly right; a horrifying thought. The league, as I was now coming to think of them, saw a way to get us into the open. It was a crazy thing to do, but I doubted they even hesitated.

In ten seconds of argument, the smoke quadrupled. The ceiling was now a haze of grey where the warm air rose as if even it sensed the need to escape. I could feel it catching in my throat when I breathed and knew it was already too late for anyone to stop. A few handheld fire extinguishers were not going to do the trick.

Dean's ex-wife, or whoever was calling the shots behind the scenes, was astute enough to see the challenge of finishing their grisly task if we all hunkered down in the restaurant. The fire would force us out, no doubt about it. But just to be sure, they cut the power too.

For the second time today, the wedding guests were plunged into darkness and, just like at the castle, screams of startlement cut through the air.

One moment I could see. The next there was nothing but inky black soup before my eyes. Instantly disorientated, a bump to my right shoulder almost sent me to the floor.

"I'm out of here!" The sound of Dean's voice going by told me who caused the collision, but he was past me and gone, activating the light on his phone to find his way out.

More puddles of light flared into life, each one forcing the darkness to retreat a little more. It was no surprise the groom ran; the mob mentality was one insane vote away from doing the league of killers' job for them.

Whether or not he intended it, the crowd reacted to follow Dean's lead.

First one, then two, then a stampede as everyone in the restaurant went for the exit. Some were fast, running to get there. Less able others were slower, but when I looked for Lily's grandmother she was no longer where she had been. Lily's father had her in his arms, his feet moving swiftly despite the load.

I found myself swept along and had to fight to get out of the way. My pets were here, and I couldn't leave without them.

Mindy shouted, "I've got Amber!" and a bark from Buster reassured my stressed heart, but my relief was momentary, replaced by fear a second later when the shooting started.

Just going through the door from the restaurant, it shocked me to find the wedding guests who went first were coming toward me and running even faster than before. I had to throw on the brakes to arrest my forward motion and reverse course. It was that or get trampled.

Two more shots rang out, driving fear through my heart. We knew who was behind the murders now and we knew why, but knowledge wouldn't save us. When no cry of pain or scream of horror arose in the wake of the shots, I prayed it meant the person with the gun was a terrible shot.

Mindy shoved me through the door and back into the restaurant. Amber clung to her chest like Velcro. Buster whipped past my feet, barking his excitement in the near total darkness. Sensing something moving ahead of me, I swung the light on my phone to find Milford and Oswald framed in the beam.

We'd left them behind, abandoning our captives to die in the fire or from smoke inhalation as everyone bomb burst for the exit. Still tied to their chairs, they were shuffling/hopping on two feet to escape.

Part of me wanted to stop to help them. I didn't like to think they might die, but I also wasn't about to untie them. My concerns faded quickly when I saw the ties used to bind their wrists and ankles were coming loose. They were battling to get free and soon would.

Much faster than me, Mindy led me around them to the kitchen where the smoke was now so thick the light from my phone struggled to penetrate it.

Coughing, and stretching her top up to cover her mouth, Mindy asked, "We can get out through here, right?"

The storeroom to the kitchen provided access to the yard outside, presumably to simplify unloading deliveries. We were at the back of the hotel now, away from the picturesque front façade. Provided the storeroom wasn't locked, we would exit to the woods Morag claimed would lead to her neighbour.

I had no clue where I was going, but the aim right now was to be somewhere else. We could figure out directions once we were away from the league of murderous maniacs.

Leading with her left shoulder, Mindy slammed into the storeroom door, and it flew open. The smoke was in my lungs, making every sip of air a hellish torture that drew hacking coughs. I needed to shout for everyone to follow me, but trying to take a deep enough breath to do so was impossible.

"Auntie! Come on!" Mindy was outside in the cold, crisp night air. Still coughing, she was at least able to breathe now.

The cold bit at my exposed skin, but the smoke began to clear, the breeze outside pulling it from the building. Sucking in some air, I was about to shout when the wedding guests streamed into the storeroom from the kitchen. They stumbled, coughing, and choking, but passing the message back to those behind. There was a way out. All they had to do was keep moving.

"Buster," I wheezed. "Stay close."

The snow was up to my knees and even deeper in places where the wind drove it. To Buster that meant he ploughed a path through it with his face. The soot that covered his fur coat was coming off, tainting the perfect white blanket with fine black particles.

"*Not going to go far,*" he mumbled, his head barely visible above the surface.

We moved away from the building to make room as more and more of the bride and groom's guests escaped the hotel. No one seemed to know what to do, but when Dean forced his way through the crowd, pushing and using his elbows to get clear, he grabbed Morag's arm.

"Which way to your neighbour's?"

Her husband tried to intervene. "Hey, take your hands off her."

Dean ignored him. "Which way!"

Morag angled her free arm through the trees. "It's that way. There's a path that starts on the other side of these trees."

Dean didn't pause to encourage Lily or anyone else to go with him. He just took off, making best speed through the snow.

Mindy pulled me after him, grabbing my hand to make me follow.

"We should put some distance between us and whoever is doing the shooting, Auntie."

"Wait," I gasped in a lungful of air. "Is everyone out?"

We looked around, trying to identify if there was anyone still inside the burning building other than members of the league.

"She's right," said Morag, reading my mind. "We should barricade these doors so they can't follow us."

It felt callous, but I think everyone realised this was a life or death situation. The cold would make our escape perilous enough. Removing a gang of crazed killers from the equation was just common sense.

Wheelie bins loaded with rubbish augmented the broom Morag wedged against the door to hold it shut. It wouldn't hold forever, but it didn't have to. The hotel was so full of smoke, anyone trapped inside would struggle to survive.

With her husband and the kids close by, Morag said, "Come on. It's this way." She was going and if we wanted a guide to find the security we all hoped her nearest neighbour could provide, we had to go too.

The guests had almost no protection from the cold and though men gave up their jackets so the women in dresses might have something to protect their bare skin, the walk through the woods was going to be tough for everyone. Hugging their arms around their bodies, couples and families huddled close. They were moving, but it was slow going.

My feet had never been so cold. With no barrier to separate them from the snow, the icy crystals chilled everything they touched. Goodness knows how Buster felt, dragging his undercarriage through the drifts.

The trudge became all-consuming. Fighting the cold and the pain it brought left no room to think of anything else.

Until the league found us.

Trudging Through the Snow

The blanket of pure, white snow reflected light from the moon and stars, making it possible to see even if it was still dark out.

When the first shot rang out, the 'crack' reverberating through the night, our sorry group was in the trees. Morag was right that there was a path, but it was barely wide enough to justify the term. Unable to walk side by side, many splintered off to walk through the trees on either side.

A second shot followed the first before anyone had time to make their bodies react. However, when it smacked into a tree in the centre of our group, it had much the same effect as dropping a bomb.

Everyone moved at once, spreading outward to get away. Running through the snow was hard, but that's what everyone did.

A scream laced with rage echoed through the night. "Dean!"

Fear drove me from the path without a glance to see who was following. Was it just Dean's deranged ex-wife, or was it all of them? Milford and Oswald were free now which, so far as I knew, meant the entire league was coming to kill us. They wanted Dean, but the wild shots into the woods told us they didn't care who they had to kill to get to him.

"Auntie!"

Until I heard Mindy's voice, I hadn't realised we were separated. She was off to my right somewhere. There were people crashing through the snow and branches ahead of me, and the path was somewhere to my rear.

Or was it?

I was completely turned about.

Buster barked, letting me know he was okay, but he wasn't with me either.

"Auntie!"

A shot rang out, and I heard Mindy swear. Cussing aloud meant she was alive, but I was convinced the shooter used her voice as an aiming mark. Returning her call would be foolish, a conclusion reached by all. Shouts to locate loved ones, family, and friends ceased in an instant, the woodland falling eerily silent.

A light whisper reached my ears. "Mrs Philips?" I twisted to find Lily closing on my position. She looked frozen. Her lips were blue and her teeth were chattering. The man's jacket she wore over her dress hung open, the warmth it might offer doing nothing. "I don't know which way to go," she sobbed, her voice a whisper lest she be heard. Save for the breeze that blew gently now, the night was still, and sound would travel. The crunch of snow came from every direction, but whether we were hearing guests running away or a killer stalking toward us, we could not tell.

Still visible through the trees, the hotel was on fire. I was far enough into the trees now that I couldn't see the building properly. A bright glow of orange light backlit it, highlighting the doomed property that now acted as a reference point.

Gripped by terror and fearful for every single wedding attendee, I could do nothing for them, but I could try to save the bride. If I did nothing else, guiding Lily to safety gave me a focus.

I nudged her shoulder, aiming my eyes away from the hotel. There were trees in every direction, their branches intertwining and overlapping to give a sense of impenetrability. Picking the direction I hoped would prove to run parallel to the path, I hoped to stay clear of that for as long as possible without actually getting lost. If I got it right, we could cut back across to find it later.

The land was flatish, so the hotel would remain in sight like a twisted north star from which I could navigate.

Trying to sound more confident than I felt, I whispered, "We're going that way. The path is to our left. We can track alongside it and regroup with people later."

I got a timid, "Okay," in response and willed my legs to get going again.

I had never been so cold in my life, and it concerned me that the pain in my feet was fading. What did that mean? Was the cold killing my nerves? Was my flesh starting to freeze? I'd read somewhere that freezing to death was an okay way to go. You just slow down and stop, kind of like falling asleep, except forever.

Wordlessly, and with Lily by my side, I forged a path through the snow.

"Walk in my footsteps," I told her. "No sense both of us struggling through the snow. It will be easier in my wake."

She nodded her understanding and fell into step behind me.

I could see people in the distance, passing through the trees where they would appear only to vanish again just as quickly. Vague snippets of voices drifted on the light breeze left behind by the storm. Were they friendly or otherwise? It was too dark to tell, so the only safe play was to avoid them.

However, when I spotted someone ahead, I could see it was a woman. She wasn't looking our way, but her size and shape made me think I was seeing Lily's bridesmaid, Tamara. I didn't call out, but angled my feet toward her. Glancing over my shoulder, I could see Lily had her head down. She looked beaten and hadn't seen the woman to our front.

Tamara, if indeed it was her, wasn't moving, which meant I closed the distance to her with every stride. Ten seconds after first spotting her, I was close enough to risk hissing or whispering her name. I was also close enough to tell it wasn't Tamara after all. The cold had to be making my brain feel slow because I couldn't identify which of the guests I could see.

By the time I figured out why, it was too late.

Standoff

We made almost no noise walking through the snow. Almost, but not nothing. The soft crunch of fresh snow compacting under our feet announced our presence, just when my slush-filled brain supplied the answer to why I didn't know the woman five yards to my front.

Suddenly hearing or sensing us, she spun around as though startled. She had a small calibre gun in her right hand and a smile on her face. It wasn't a friendly smile. It spoke of hate and revenge and joy at having two victims present themselves for slaughter.

Unlike everyone else, she was dressed for the cold. A proper coat, trousers, boots, and gloves would keep her warm while the rest of us froze to death. Heck, she didn't even have to shoot us. Much longer at this temperature and we were done for.

"Lily," she identified the bride. "So nice to finally meet you."

Lily stepped out from behind my back, coming to my side where she met the woman's gaze. Her eyes possessed the unfocused look I would associate with concussion. She was conscious, but cognitive reasoning and survival instincts were taking a break.

Lily said, "Hello."

The gun shifted a degree or so until it pointed at the bride's centre of mass.

"I don't want you," the woman said. "I want Dean, but I think I can use you to make him show his face."

"Agatha?" I believed I was talking to the groom's ex-wife, a guess her reaction confirmed. "Agatha, Dean won't come back for Lily. He left her behind to escape you. There is nothing to gain by hurting her."

She believed me, that much was clear from the angry set of her jaw, but my attempt to talk her into leaving Lily be did not work.

"Then I guess I'll just shoot her. Dean married me," Agatha growled. "He said his marriage vows to me. He doesn't get to just marry someone else and live happily ever after. If I can't kill him, I can take away his bride."

Thinking she was about to do it, I threw my arms up and stepped in front of Lily. Don't ask me what was going through my head, I couldn't possibly give you an answer, but too cold to think straight, I was now the bride's human shield.

Agatha narrowed her eyes. "Get out of the way."

I held my ground and she shrugged. "Fine, I guess I need to kill you anyway." Extending her arm, she levelled it at my face. I was staring down the actual barrel of a gun with nothing I could do to stop her from ending my life.

Would I even register the sensation if she shot me in the head?

"*Dun, dun, DAH!*"

Buster bounded through the snow, achieving an impressive speed since he had to leap with every pace to get above the surface like a porpoise leaping from the water.

"*I am one with the darkness*," he barked at Agatha. "*A shadow of doom from which there is no escape.*"

She shot him.

I could barely feel my arms, but snug inside her winter clothes, Agatha's limbs responded to the commands she sent. Twisting her body, she had aimed the gun and pulled the trigger.

My heart stopped working.

It restarted when my dog turned tail to run away.

She looked ready to fire again, but didn't, lifting her gun hand so the weapon pointed skyward. She watched to make sure Buster didn't circle back before turning to look at me again.

My reprieve from execution lasted but a moment. On a warm day I would have run away taking Lily with me. We would be moving targets and far harder to hit, but my feet were quite literally frozen to the spot.

Agatha pointed the gun at my head again. Should I close my eyes? Would that make it better for me? I let them flutter shut, filling my head with images of Vince and my pets. Of Mindy and my late husband.

"Hey!" said Mindy.

My eyes flicked open, desperate to see my ninja niece flatten Dean's murderous ex-wife, but I was to be disappointed.

Mindy had her arms up in surrender, her nunchucks nowhere in sight. We formed a triangle now, Agatha on one corner, Lily and me on another with Mindy fifteen yards to my left forming the third. Her arrival created a new dynamic and a problem for Agatha. We were too far apart for Agatha to cover us at the same time and, in theory, one of us might have the time to rush her if she shot the other.

In theory, but it would have to be Mindy doing the rushing. I could try, but there was no sensation left in my legs and I feared I might fall flat on my face if I tried to take a step.

Agatha saw it too and decided. She was going to shoot Mindy first, but her change in physical stance betrayed her intentions. In the half second it took for her gun to track across to my niece, Mindy bunched her muscles and dived. The bullet flew into the night and Mindy scrambled to get behind a tree.

Agatha kept glancing at me, checking I hadn't moved, but her focus was on the new danger my niece presented.

Mindy shot from her hiding place to the next tree, Agatha wasting another bullet when she missed again.

"Too slow!" Mindy taunted. Darting from tree to tree was a great tactic, but not one that would ever get her close enough to tackle Agatha before she could deliver the kill shot. Knowing that, Agatha didn't bother to shoot the next time Mindy exposed herself to get closer.

Instead, Agatha aimed her gun at me again.

"Show yourself or I shoot both of them. I assume they mean something to you."

"No, Mindy! Save yourself! Get away from here and look after my pets!"

Mindy disobeyed me. Stepping out again, she didn't bother to raise her hands, but said, "No, Auntie. I think you should continue to look after Buster and Amber. Besides, we are about to win."

Agatha snorted a laugh and pointed the gun at Mindy again. "Really? You have two seconds to live. Any last words?"

Mindy said, "Sure. Now."

"Now?" Agatha repeated. "Now what?"

Mindy flared her eyes. "Now!"

Agatha straightened her gun arm. "If you insist. Now it is."

I saw her finger tighten on the trigger, the world standing still as life or death became a race against time. Would she be able to complete the action before Morag's determined swing ended the standoff?

I first spotted the hotelier moving through the trees behind Agatha when Buster made his appearance. Deployed to sneak up on Agatha, Buster and Mindy were there to keep the killer distracted. It worked, but to approach through the snow without being heard demanded stealth, and that meant going slow.

The branch in her hands was three feet long and two inches thick. Holding it like a baseball bat, the robust Scottish woman carved an arc through the air at Agatha's head height. She never saw it coming, but while the aim was true, the timing was not.

The branch struck Agatha on the right side of her head about level with her ear. With a shower of wooden splinters showing how much energy the blow delivered, Agatha's head shifted left. It took her whole body with it, the petite woman flying through the air to crash into the snow on her side, but not before she pulled the trigger.

Unable to do anything but watch, my soul left my body. Rooted to the spot, I saw Mindy tumble backward and away. It was too dark to see the spray of blood, but the question about whether my legs were still working got answered when I raced to my niece's side.

In this instance, racing meant a speed barely above a walk, but it was the fastest I could go.

Buster came running from the other direction, both of us converging on Mindy's position just as she sat up.

She patted her body. "Dear Lord, I thought she was going to hit me."

"You're not hit!" My heart dared to beat again.

Mindy put a hand in the snow and pushed herself off the ground. "Nope. Looks like I'm fine."

Morag stood over Agatha, the branch dangling from her right hand.

Agatha wasn't moving, but a quick check of her pulse confirmed she was still alive, even if she was now bleeding into the snow from a cut to her head.

Mindy looked about for the gun but couldn't find it. Dismissing it as a problem for another day, she tapped my shoulder and pointed.

"Someone is coming."

There were in fact three someones, each carrying a torch to light their way.

A deep, booming voice cut through the air.

"Police. Call out if you can hear us."

Aftermath

We were the first people the police reached. Two constables in uniform and a detective sergeant called Stone had arrived a few minutes ago. The fire at the hotel was such that they could see it long before they arrived. It made them want to drive faster, but attempting speed in the snow would be foolhardy, so they took their time, arrived in one piece, and then started running around.

They found us when they discovered footprints leading around the side of the hotel. Barricading the exit from the storeroom forced the league to find a different way out, but confusingly, DS Stone claimed they found only one set of footprints. Small ones.

Following those, they came across dozens more when they reached the back of the hotel. That led them into the woods along the path to the point where we all took off in different directions. They had been discussing which set to follow when they heard the shot and made a beeline for our location.

Regardless of whether there were still members of Agatha's league waiting to attack us, the danger the cold represented could not be underestimated.

DS Stone sent the constables to round up the rest of the guests and placed a call to have a helicopter fly in with supplies – the storm was passing, which made flight possible. When Morag's family joined us with Amber tucked inside the girl's top, the detective led us back to the hotel with Agatha's limp form over one shoulder. From the size of the orange bloom filling the sky around the beautiful old building, there was no doubt in my mind it was beyond hope of saving.

The sight filled me with a sense of desperate misery, but the snow around the inferno was melting and if we got close enough the warmth was wonderful. DS Stone produced blankets from the Land Rover squad car and invited us to sit inside. There wasn't room for us all, but the kids and Lily could squeeze along the back seat.

More of the guests returned over the next few minutes, each with their own terrible tale of their flight through the woodland and battle against the elements. There were too few blankets to go around, so we shared, forming groups to huddle and share what little body heat we could claim. The fire helped, though with Morag and her family crying over the loss of their home and livelihood, no one celebrated the heat beating back the worst of the winter.

Guests continued to find their way to the front of the hotel, the count getting close to the full number in my head when Dean appeared. He was the last one to make it back.

He tried to talk to Lily, but was blocked from doing so by her bridesmaids, her father, her grandmother and most of the guests whether from her side of the list or his. No one wanted to share a blanket with him either, which meant he got one of his own.

Shunned, he took himself to one side and kept quiet.

All was quiet until a bark of surprise made us all turn to look away from the hotel.

Coming from the road and looking half dead from the cold, Oswald and Milford approached with their hands held up in surrender.

Now back with us, the constables apprehended the two men who were glad to be taken into custody. Breaking free from their bonds, neither man pursued the revenge that drove them to join Agatha's league. They opted instead to evade justice by running away, but a few minutes in the arctic temperatures turned them around.

What became of the rest of the league we had no idea, but when the police could find no further footprints leading away from the hotel, the natural assumption that they perished inside was the only one we could draw.

It took half an hour for the mountain rescue helicopter to arrive, the descending aircraft showering us in fresh icy particles when it landed in the field on the other side of the road. However, it came with more blankets, hot coffee, and medical supplies, though the only person needing them was Agatha.

A trio of paramedics triaged the hypothermic guests, identified those most in danger and took them first. The destination was not, however, a hospital as one might imagine, but the nearest building in which we could shelter.

Flown to the other end of the lake five at a time, the helicopter delivered us to another hotel, one which had no available rooms, but was going to put us up all the same. Like evacuees from a natural disaster or survivors from a ship that sunk, the hotel staff rallied to make us comfortable. A conference centre became our dormitory for the night, the carpet our mattress, but it was warm and safe, and the kitchen produced food.

The police stayed with us, DS Stone asking questions and taking details only once we were settled, comfortable and ready to do so. They housed Milford and Oswald elsewhere, the constables taking turns to watch them.

Amber and Buster tucked themselves up between me and Mindy, content to sleep until the morning. We were both too tired to waste effort or energy dissecting the events of the day.

In the morning, I awoke stiff and sore from sleeping on the hard floor, but like everyone else, it seemed, I had come through the ordeal without injury.

There was breakfast for us, though not in the hotel's restaurant as that was full catering to their paying guests. Bacon sandwiches, hot tea, and buttered toast ensured no one went hungry, but now we needed to return to the Loch Richmond Hotel and Spa to collect our cars. That was going to be a problem for some as their keys were in their rooms.

Mercifully, I had mine.

Snowploughs in the night meant the roads around the loch were now clear. It was so odd that a few hours ago getting anywhere was impossible, and now salt on the tarmac made it look no different from any other day.

It took another few hours to get the car and return to the castle where Philippe could not have been more pleased to see us. From there we had to drive to the hospital to collect Justin. He wore a bandage around his head, though he expressed how unnecessary he believed it to be. Cleared to leave, he did not have a concussion. In fact, his only wound was a small cut where the blow struck his skull. Justin was fine to travel and, like the rest of us, wanted nothing other than to go home.

So that was what we did.

Elizabeth Keats

E lizabeth cursed her way back to the bed-and-breakfast. It had all been so promising. The plan went so well to start with. How had it ended with failure?

After killing the man who looked dead even before she stabbed him, she accepted defeat. Felicity was nowhere to be seen and every minute she stayed at the hotel, the more likely it was that she would get caught.

Hating that she was giving up and that Felicity not only still had the contract for the royal wedding but was very much still alive, she donned her winter clothes and took the snowmobile across the snowy landscape.

The couple at the bed-and-breakfast were shocked to see her. Just like at the hotel, she hid the snowmobile behind a hedge and walked the last quarter mile. It allowed her to claim she was walking when the storm hit, providing a story that accounted for her day.

They warmed her before their fire, made her food, and checked constantly to see if there was anything she needed. In the morning she would travel home, returning to her life and her own wedding planner business. No one would ever know she had been in Scotland and if one ignored the arson and vandalism, she hadn't committed a crime. Certainly not the one she intended.

I mean, sure she murdered a man, but he looked dead anyway and she had no idea who he was, so it hardly counted.

There was still time. That was what Elizabeth told herself. The royal wedding was still almost four months away. Devoid of a backup plan, the need to kill Felicity Philips remained in place and she was just going to have to come up with something new.

Epilogue

The following day, snuggled on the sofa with Buster on one side and Amber on the other, I was going through my list of suppliers for the royal wedding when someone knocked at the front door. Having taken a few days off to be with me, Vince was in my kitchen fixing tea.

"I'll get it," he called on his way through the house.

Amber didn't open her eyes, but said, "*Another interruption? Taking a nap anywhere in your vicinity is irritating, Felicity.*"

I took my eyes from the laptop to cast them at her. "You haven't moved in hours, Amber. What interruptions are you referring to?"

"*You got up when the postman came.*"

"That was more than an hour ago, Amber."

"*Precisely. That was an interruption, and this is another one. What part of my statement are you finding fault with?*"

Dismissing her concerns, I could hear Vince talking to someone at the door. More than one someone in fact.

I folded my laptop and placed it on the coffee table. Vince was inviting my visitors inside, and I wanted to be standing to greet them. Thinking it might be neighbours or an old friend – Vince wouldn't let the press cross my threshold, I was surprised to see DI Cassie Rush, the detective inspector from the palace. It wasn't just her though, she had three uniformed officers with her and when I glanced outside I could see even more. The ones in my front garden carried firearms.

I would have asked what was going on had an unmarked police car not swept past the front of my house. The black Range Rover tailing it turned into my driveway and I could guess who was hidden behind the blacked-out windows.

A second unmarked police car pulled up behind the first, blocking the Range Rover in. Officers in uniform opened the back doors.

DI Rush controlled it all with commands over the radio.

As Prince Marcus and Nora Morley stepped from the back seat, DI Rush looked my way.

"Sorry about the intrusion. Secrecy is of paramount importance, so we could not call in advance to announce the visit."

"I would have come to you."

DI Rush said, "This is more expedient."

Buster tried to get out, his stumpy tail wagging hard even after I caught his collar.

"Stay with me, Buster. I doubt they are here to see you."

The prince and his fiancé were always smiling in pictures captured by the press and were one of the cutest couples it had ever been my pleasure to work with. Today they looked troubled.

A small sigh escaped me. They were here to call off the wedding, or postpone it, or otherwise dash my plans. That could have been done over the phone, or by summoning me to the palace and it spoke volumes about their class that they came to me to deliver the bad news in person.

After the recent run of royal deaths and rumours that there might be someone behind it, I had to admit I wasn't entirely surprised and prayed they would push the date and keep me on rather than put it on hold indefinitely.

I had it all wrong though.

Sitting opposite them in my living room, I was unprepared for the request the prince delivered.

"In four weeks," I repeated.

"That is correct. Can you do it, Mrs Philips?" Prince Marcus was genuinely asking me, not making a demand.

Instead of four months, I now had four weeks. Four weeks to pull off the biggest and most prestigious wedding of my career. It was impossible. It was ridiculous.

I was going to do it.

For months, DI Cassie Rush acted as the lone voice raising concerns that the royal family were in danger. It started when Nugent Chamberlain, thirteenth in line to the throne died in the flaming wreckage of a flying dragon suit. She maintained his death was intended to misdirect the police and that his killer was therefore still at large.

She suspected Nugent's brother, who Mindy had been dating for months. Lacking evidence, she had nothing with which she could justify a full investigation. Nevertheless, her superiors were now listening, and they were worried about Prince Marcus's imminent nuptials. The royal family would all be in one place at the same time. If ever there was going to be a strike against them, that was when it would happen.

So in utter secrecy, the date was being brought forward by three months. There would be no announcement until the day. Visiting dignitaries and celebrities arriving in England would give the game away, but only in the final day or so before the event. There was a ruse ready to throw the press and general public off the scent, but I had to play my part. My movements had to cloud the change of date, not highlight it or give anyone cause to question if there might be something afoot.

My suppliers would need to sign non-disclosure agreements and drop whatever they were doing to meet the adjusted timeline. It made my head reel from the information overload. It swam with thoughts as I tried to plan my way around the challenge, even while DI Rush and the prince were still talking to me about what had to happen next.

My budget, which had always been generous, was now effectively unlimited. If I pulled this off, it would be the single greatest piece of wedding planning in the history of the planet.

When they were gone and I was alone with Vince a short while later, he said, "You're going to need more help."

He wasn't wrong, but calling in backup to manage the reduced timeline had been my first consideration. It was all a bit terrifying, as was the first call.

"Why are you calling me?" demanded Primrose Green.

Rivals for years, she was a talented wedding planner who knew she was second to me. Dirty tactics to undermine my work rather than working harder to outdo me had often been her preferred strategy, but I had no time to dwell on that now. I needed her help and there was no chance she might turn down my request that she come on board.

"This isn't a trick?" she questioned, doubt dripping from every word.

I couldn't tell her about the change of date, not until she signed an NDA, but I promised my offer was genuine and that she would get to claim credit for her part. With her on board, I dialled the next number.

"Felicity?"

"Patricia, I need your help."

Others might have asked what for and guarded their commitment. Patricia Fisher had a simpler response.

"When and where?"

I outlined what little I could tell her without embellishing my need for her skills. The call lasted less than two minutes, ending with her confirming she would return to England in less than a month.

I sighed with relief to know she was on board and looked up the last number on my mental list.

When it was first announced that the prince's wedding would not be handled by the royal household, and firms such as mine were asked to bid for the role, I could only see two others as my competition. Primrose was one. The other was a woman I had never viewed as a serious rival, but if I considered her to be the third best in the county, I was acknowledging her talent and determination.

The phone rang and connected.

"Elizabeth Keats."

The End

Book 10 is waiting for you at the click of the link. Scan the QR code with your phone to find your copy of The Royal Wedding.

Book 10 is waiting for you at the click of the link. Scan the QR code with your phone to find your copy of The Royal Wedding.

Author's Notes:

H ello, Dear Reader,

Thank you for reaching the end of the book with me. This one was fun to write, but I say that about almost all my books and this series has proven to be more fun than most. This is the penultimate story in this series, the next being the concluding episode that will tie off the loose ends and close the subplots while leaving a fun little question mark in your heads.

I realise that is cryptic, but it will make sense when you get there. The final book is set to be written in four books' time. If you wonder why, I am afraid to say it is because you have not been paying attention.

Felicity and pals are just one set of characters within a greater universe. In the final book, Patricia Fisher, Albert Smith, and the Blue Moon Investigations team will join her, all of which you have met while reading her stories. They each have subplots within their stories that lead them to the royal wedding. It is that subplot that forms the basis of Felicity's series and the backdrop for her grand finale.

To that end, now that I have finished this story, I must write a complete tale for each of the other series to deliver their characters to the royal wedding. There they will each pursue their own thread to meet each other in a climatic showdown that is so incredible inside my fractured brain that I would probably go insane if I had the slightest idea what I was doing.

A few items of note about this story: One thing to reveal is that I was a choirboy at our local church for many, many years. Or so it seemed at the time. I joined the army at seventeen though, so I was probably in the choir for less than a decade. My point is that during that time I attended a lot of weddings. Often the happy couple would request the choir and we would show up on a Saturday, sometimes for two or three or even four weddings one after the other. *Love Divine All Loves Excelling*, was requested for just about every single one of them, and I can still remember every line forty years after the last time I sang it.

Needless to say, it was not a choice opted for when I married my lady.

I served for many years with Scottish infantry and calvary units during my time as a soldier. It took a while to discern different accents and pick out one from another. In the beginning, I would stare in bewilderment when they hurled a stream of words in my direction, questioning if they had just told me a joke or threatened to start a fight. However, many years into my career I found myself in Glasgow in the company of a US Army Colonel for whom I had to act as interpreter. I guess I picked something up along the way.

Picturing the boy band, I had in mind the lead singer from *A Flock of Seagulls*. Readers of a certain age will remember them. The eighties were an era of silly haircuts, but few could rival that sported by Mike Score. If you cannot picture him, just put the band's name into your search engine.

It is late in November, just a few days before my fifty-fourth birthday. The weather outside is turning cold, but it is warm in my house. For the first winter in many years, I will not freeze every day, hunched over my keyboard in the log cabin at the bottom of my garden, for I have a newly built office inside our house in which to remain comfortable.

My little girl was diagnosed with autism a week ago, but we already knew she was neurodivergent. The diagnosis allows us to engage the additional support services we need to help her realise her best potential.

Chances are Hermione will grow up to be an astronaut or a tech wizard. Her brain is wired differently, but her uniqueness will give her an edge over her contemporaries. It is down to me and my wife to ensure she gets what she needs to be her best self.

The future is full of opportunity and potential.

Take care.

Steve Higgs

What's next for Felicity?

A Royal Wedding. Pomp, pageantry, and a healthy portion of psychotic killers ...

For Felicity Philips, wedding planner to the rich and famous, this is her dream job, but convinced someone is out to wreck the whole thing, her attention is on keeping everyone alive.

There is security in place, hundreds of cops and bodyguards assigned to the royal family, but do any of them know the threat is coming from multiple angles?

A party of antiroyalists have been plotting for years, one of Felicity's rivals wants nothing more than to see her competitor fail in her greatest moment, and a member of the British royal family has their eyes set firmly on the throne. All they must do is remove everyone in their path to get there. What better time to take them out than when they are all together?

Mercifully for Felicity, she is not alone. Certain of her need for help she has enlisted super sleuth Patricia Fisher, but her old friend is not the only detective at the event. Albert Smith is an honoured guest of the king. He's there with his trusted canine sidekick and they encountered the antiroyalists months ago. Finally, Tempest Michaels and the Blue Moon team have followed their own trail of clues to the wedding. They think they might know the identity of the murderous royal, but proving it, accusing a member of the royal household, is not a task one approaches without absolute certainty.

In the climatic conclusion to Felicity Philip's series, all the players will come together, their stories intertwining as the righteous battle the greedy, the corrupt, and the morally insane.

What does a wedding planner know about organising the greatest wedding ever witnessed?

Everything.

Absolutely everything.

Free books and more

Want to see what else I have written? Go to my website.

https://stevehiggsbooks.com/

Or sign up to my newsletter where you will get sneak peeks, exclusive giveaways, behind the scenes content, and more. Plus, you'll be notified of Fan Pricing events when they occur and get exclusive offers from other authors because all UF writers are automatically friends.

Click the link or copy it carefully into your web browser.

https://stevehiggsbooks.com/newsletter/

Prefer social media? Join my thriving Facebook community.

Want to join the inner circle where you can keep up to date with everything? This is a free group on Facebook where you can hang out with likeminded individuals and enjoy discussing my books. There is cake too (but only if you bring it).

https://www.facebook.com/groups/1151907108277718

Printed in Great Britain
by Amazon

55590626R00128